STORM AND FIRE

STORM AND FIRE

KELLY ADAMS

Five Star • Waterville, Maine

Five Star Romance Series.

Published in 2002 in conjunction with Maureen Moran Agency.

The text of this edition is unabridged.

Set in 11 pt. Plantin by Minnie B. Raven.

Printed in the United States on permanent paper.

ISBN 0-7862-4158-6 (hc : alk. paper)

STORM AND FIRE

CHAPTER ONE

Emma Henley Kendrick could spot trouble a mile away, and here it was, she thought wryly as she pushed open the door to her sister's kitchen.

Sunny was on the phone, and Emma recognized that slightly petulant frown and cupid-bow pursing of the lips all too well. Sunny was working on a man again. Emma wondered what was going on now and, more importantly, how it would involve her. Because, knowing Sunny, it would.

Sunny's brows were knitting in irritation, and the girlish lilt had faded from her voice. "Now listen here, Mr. Rivers," she said sharply, apparently trading all her wiles for the direct approach. "What's going on here? I heard that you punched my son's coach in a bar, and now you call and say that Cory got in trouble and he's moved in with you."

Uh-oh, Emma thought, sitting down at the table and depositing her purse on the floor. For once in her life, Sunny appeared to be in over her head if the betraying wail in her voice was an accurate indication. Cory was Sunny's ten-year-old son, and at the moment he was spending his summer vacation at an expensive football camp in Maryland. "Well, if he turns pro when he grows up, think of the great men his old mom will hobnob with," Sunny had explained when Emma questioned her. Sunny was one of those optimistic women who believed in being prepared for any of life's more exotic opportunities.

Sunny had dealt with a lot of men in her life, and none of them ever knew what had hit him. In Emma's eyes,

Sunny was the Venus's-flytrap of womankind. Sweet and pretty, she all but devoured her conquests alive, bewitching them with wide blue eyes and a voice that could grow pure cane sugar. Not that she was heartless. Quite the contrary. But the two sisters were the children of overworked, underpaid Reverend Horace Henley. Their father's position in the tiny Iowa community of Parton, plus his obvious affection for his daughters, had bred in each girl a certain resourcefulness. Sunny dipped into her ever-flowing well of charm when there was something she wanted, while Emma, ever the more forthright of the two, resorted to stubbornness instead. Sunny's blue eyes would glow and sparkle with coquettish lights while Emma's genetically identical ones would fix steadfastly and solemnly on the subject of her attention. "Don't let those big eyes fool you," the girls' Aunt Charlotte would warn their father. "Those two are terrors inside. Lord help the men who tangle with them."

Over the years the two had come to each other's rescue on every occasion that demanded rescuing—broken dates, broken curfews, and broken hearts. More often, it was Sunny who courted trouble and Emma who sniffed it out, then set about righting it.

"Here, you talk to him!" Sunny said abruptly, pushing the phone toward her sister.

Emma started and shook her head. "I don't even know what's going on here."

A muffled male voice could be heard on the phone, and Sunny answered it in annoyance. "Just hold the insults a minute. I'm putting my sister on."

"If that's a threat, you're waving an empty gun," Emma said reasonably as the phone was thrust at her again. "I don't know how I can help if I haven't the slightest idea who's on the other end."

"Joel Rivers," Sunny hissed. "He's the father of Cory's friend Mike at camp."

"And what's his horrible crime?" Emma asked calmly.

Sunny rolled her eyes in exasperation. "Weren't you listening? The man got into a drunken brawl and now Cory's living with him. And he has the nerve to tell me *Cory's* in trouble."

"I thought Cory had to stay in the camp dorm," Emma said, trying to digest this.

"He did, but he got kicked out somehow. Something else this Mr. Rivers was involved in. Emma, you have to go out there and get Cory."

"What?" Emma stared in disbelief at her sister. Sunny took advantage of her momentary paralysis to put the phone in Emma's hand. The annoyed male voice was still vibrating in the receiver as Emma dumbly held it to her ear.

"—don't care much about your son's welfare," the annoyed voice was saying, and to her irritation Emma felt a pleasurable sensation in her stomach at the timbre of that deep, husky tone. It was irritation mixed with indignation as he continued, oblivious to the fact that Sunny was no longer listening. "So if you want to know how Cory's doing, then I suggest you get your tail out here and see for yourself, Mrs. Walters, and quit trying to monitor your kid's life by telephone." The broad *o* in his accent was both regional and arrogant.

Emma cleared her throat and stood up, hoping she could sound intimidating. "Have you finished your tirade, Mr.—" She glanced at Sunny for the name. "—Rivers, or do you have some more suggestions as to what I can do with my tail?" Sunny stifled what was either a cough or a guffaw.

There was a brief silence from the other end of the conversation, and then a suspicious voice said, "And who are you—Mrs. Walters' henchlady?"

"I'm Sunny's sister, Emma Kendrick. And you're the drunken brawler, I presume?"

There was definite irritation in his voice when he answered. "Oh, yes, ma'am. That's me."

His voice was deep and gravelly, and Emma quelled the quicksilver rush of warmth feathering down to her thighs. She shouldn't be feeling this way. Somehow her brain had jumbled its emotional circuits. She was in reality supposed to be annoyed with this man, and the insistent tingle racing through her blood was a mistake of her nervous system.

Emma caught a glimpse of herself in the mirrored tiles over the stove. Impatiently, she ran a hand through her short, toast-brown hair, and the tangle of bangs on her forehead settled back into disarray. Her chin jutted at a determined angle, but that was softened by the soft curve of her mouth and the openness in her wide blue eyes. Emma frowned and looked away.

"Mr. Rivers," she said crisply, "Sunny hasn't given me any coherent explanation of her dispute with you, and you seem more concerned with tossing off insults."

"Ms. Kendrick, are you married?" he demanded.

"What?"

"I asked if you're married."

"I don't see that that's any of your concern, Mr. Rivers, and it has nothing to do with the matter at hand."

"I wasn't proposing, Ms. Kendrick," he said dryly. "I just asked for information. Because if you're not, then that explains a lot. You and your sister seem to lack certain basic maternal instincts."

Emma's blood came to a boil and prepared an assault on her skin, rapidly turning it pink. "If this is a sample of your technique with women, Mr. Rivers, then I assume that you're not married either."

"Wait a minute!" he said. "You're Aunt Emma, aren't you? The one who dry-cleaned Cory's hamster?"

Oh, God. No one in the family had ever let her forget that episode with the dry shampoo. Heaven knew what else Cory had been telling this obnoxious man. His voice was a degree warmer than before though, and to her dismay Emma felt her knees weakening enough to make her want to sit down. She fought the urge.

"I don't want to talk about hamsters," she said determinedly. "I think Cory ought to come home." She heard his intake of breath on the other end and guessed he was frowning. "Just how is Cory?"

"He's . . . okay," he said. "He's staying with Mike and me now. He got into some trouble with a store, and the camp . . . well, they asked him to leave the dorm."

"What kind of trouble?" Emma demanded, frowning. This didn't sound like Cory.

"He was caught shoplifting." His voice wasn't unkind, and Emma fought to keep from giving herself up to the dark attraction she felt. "Apparently it had happened a couple of times before, and this time the store decided to notify the camp."

Emma ran a hand through her hair. "That's not like Cory," she said worriedly.

"Maybe you don't know him as well as you think, Ms. Kendrick," he suggested sarcastically. "As I told your sister, you can't mother a boy long distance."

Emma tightened her grip on the telephone. This man was arrogant and presumptuous! He was a stranger, and he was adopting this patronizing tone with her and announcing that she and Sunny weren't doing a very good job with Cory. Well, the hell with that.

11

This had been a rough year for Sunny. A new baby and a divorce within a few months of each other. The Henley women were cursed, doomed never to be lucky in love, according to Aunt Charlotte; so far she'd been proved right. Emma had been widowed three years ago, and now Sunny was divorced.

Emma was beginning to get a headache. Men always seemed to give you a headache.

"Mr. Rivers, I think Cory should come home," Emma said decisively. "Obviously things aren't working out there."

"That would be a mistake, Ms. Kendrick," he said immediately. "I think Cory's better off right here."

Emma almost blurted out an expletive, but years of biting her tongue in deference to her father stopped her in time. "I don't think you should be the judge of that," she snapped.

"And you're not here with Cory," he countered, "so I have to be the judge right now, Ms. Kendrick."

My God! She'd need medicine for hypertension before she finished with Mr. Joel Rivers! "Look, Mr. Rivers," she said, all patience exhausted, "Cory's coming home, and that's final. I'll talk to Sunny and make the arrangements."

"Gee, Ms. Kendrick, does this mean I won't get to talk to you anymore?" he asked sarcastically.

"Try to contain your disappointment, Mr. Rivers," she said with all the warmth of the North Pole, and promptly hung up on him.

"Well, did you get it straightened out?" Sunny asked brightly from the door, cradling a sleepy baby Melinda in one arm. "I knew Cory couldn't really be in any trouble."

"Sunny, it would take a two-hundred-pound steam iron to get the wrinkles out of this mess," she said emphatically. At the moment Emma had no tolerance for Sunny's talent for sweeping anything disagreeable under a mental rug.

"Oh, Emma, you know how good you are at dealing with people," Sunny assured her, pouring them each a glass of iced tea. "Just look at how efficiently you handle the county fuel assistance program."

"Number One, it's June, and the fuel assistance program is on hiatus," Emma said, taking her glass and sitting at the table. "And Number Two, massaging my ego isn't going to get you out of this one."

Sunny stopped jiggling the fussing baby. "That Mr. Rivers certainly acted like a Number Two, didn't he?" she said, and Emma couldn't help grinning. Sunny shifted Melinda to her shoulder and patted her back, a wry smile touching her mouth. "His voice sounded sexy though."

"Sunny!"

"Oh, come on, Emma. It's time you took an interest in men again."

"Mr. Rivers is the last person I'd want to get interested in," Emma assured her.

"Hell, honey, you have to take a chance sometime. I know things weren't good between you and Paul before he died, but—Oh, damn! Now I sound like I believe in that stupid Henley Family Curse Aunt Charlotte always talks about: generations of hapless females fated to love men who don't love them back."

"And all because some clumsy European ancestor spilled her grog on a hot-tempered gypsy. Or so legend goes." Emma sighed. "Poor Dad. A family story like that must be an embarrassment to a minister."

"I can't say that our luck has been so hot, kid. Look at us. I'm divorced with Cory and a baby, and you're widowed with a general store that might as well be ten babies for all the energy it takes."

Emma traced a line down the sweating glass of iced tea. "I'm behind on the mortgage payments again, and Mr. Calhoun at the bank is after me to sell. He says he has a buyer."

"Then sell! For heaven's sake, Emma, it's far too much work for you to handle. There's no point in driving yourself into the ground. You'll wind up in the hospital again."

"I know. But it's hard to let it go. Paul was so proud of the place."

"Em, Paul's been gone for three years now. And it's like you're doing some penance, tying yourself down to that store, struggling to make ends meet when they're never even going to get within hollering distance. You told me Paul talked about a divorce before he died, and it's like you're hanging onto that store to prove something to yourself."

"It's hard to let go," Emma said lightly, but it was a question she'd asked herself night after weary night. What was she doing it for? It was all she had left, she supposed.

"Well, I have the cure you need," Sunny said and grinned.

"Now why don't I want to hear what you're going to say?"

"Really, Em, you'd have fun. You could make a vacation of it. Rest and sightsee a couple of days in Maryland, right on the Chesapeake Bay. Cory says it's beautiful. And then you could bring him home."

"And what about football camp?"

"So he'll pick it up in high school." Sunny shrugged. "I can wait a while to shake my pompoms."

"I can't spare the time now," Emma said.

14

Sunny snorted. "And when are you going to find time for yourself? Take it now, Em. Aunt Charlotte can rustle up a couple of guys to help out at the store. And you know how Dad loves to get in there. He says he writes his best sermons after mingling with the general populace."

Emma smiled wryly. She had no doubt that their aunt would round up more than enough help, though how competent they would be was dubious. Aunt Charlotte worked in the bakery section of a grocery store, and she was famous for two skills—her cake icing talent and her arm-twisting brand of persuasion. And it was true that the Reverend Henley wrote powerful sermons after a day selling work boots, comic books, and ice-cream cones from Emma's assorted stock. But this wasn't vacation time for Emma they were talking about. As usual, Sunny was sending her sister into the fray to settle a family matter.

"Okay," Emma said dispiritedly. "I'll go beat Mr. Joel Rivers to a pulp for you."

" 'Atta girl!" Sunny crowed. "Here. Burp your niece while I microwave us a pizza."

Melinda waved her fists in the air as Emma took her from Sunny, and Emma tickled her chin with one finger. "So what do you think, sweet baby?" she asked. "I'm not going to run into trouble on your mommy's errand, am I?"

Melinda gave a loud burp, and spit up a little formula. Emma sighed.

CHAPTER TWO

There was no direct route to Thorn Haven, Maryland, Emma discovered as she stopped her car on a narrow dirt road that barely qualified as a trail. This wasn't what she had expected at all.

She had managed to get her things in order in two days, and Aunt Charlotte had come through with two young men who had grown up working in stores and were—blessed relief!—more than willing to help out. Sunny had volunteered, after a bit of figurative arm-twisting by Emma, to take over as children's choir director and Sunday school teacher in Emma's absence. So Emma had packed her clothes and loaded the car. She'd debated about calling Joel Rivers to let him know she was coming, but in the end she'd decided against it. After their last conversation, she had learned that not much could be resolved over the phone with Mr. Rivers.

Now she was wondering if Thorn Haven might be mythical after all. She stared at the map Sunny had given her. Readability was not improved by the glob of pizza sauce her sister had dropped in the middle of the Chesapeake Bay. And Sunny had been typically vague. "I didn't actually see Thorn Haven," she told Emma. "The boys all met in Baltimore, and a bus took them from there. But I have a nice brochure." Emma, unwilling to face the prospect of a harrowing search through Sunny's cluttered kitchen drawers, had told her to forget the brochure.

Emma sighed and put the map down. The man at the

gas station had told her to take the next right turn and stay on the road, and that's what she'd done. But here she was, her tires just inches away from marshy ground melting into a large body of sparkling blue-green water on the right side and brushing thick, rampant brambles on the left.

She opened the car door, shutting it partially as she got out, and inched around the encroaching weeds. Raising a hand to her forehead, she scanned the wild landscape. Something bit her on the leg and she smacked at it. The hum of insects was a counterpoint to the steady lapping of water. The water was beautiful and hypnotic, and she watched it for a long time, conscious of how different the land here was from Iowa. She was used to the bold golds and blues of fields and never-ending sky. What she had expected here was city after city. But crossing the Chesapeake Bay Bridge was like entering another country. There was water everywhere—creeks and rivers with French, English, and Indian names and the magnificent Chesapeake itself. She had passed houses along the shoreline that were originally English manors, homes built before the Revolutionary War. Where Iowa was like a rich bolt of cloth unfurled as far as the eye could see, this Chesapeake country was a labyrinth of fabrics stitched together—colors and textures and details that changed and surprised at every turn.

But where the heck was Thorn Haven hiding?

A sudden disturbance in the trees startled her, and she gave a cry and stepped backward as something large and brown rose from the top of a nearby tree with a great thrashing of leaves. She saw that it was some kind of bird, about two feet in length, with a wingspan of more than four feet. Its underside was pure white with dramatic brown markings. It glided away over the water, and Emma glanced back at the tree. Then she saw the sign she'd missed before—FERRY—with an arrow pointing straight ahead. The sign was handmade and obviously not meant to provide more than minimal guidance, and Emma climbed back in the car. Maybe whoever ran the ferry could tell her where Thorn Haven was. She had the beginning of a headache, and she rubbed her forehead mechanically as she watched the bird suddenly swoop to the surface of the water, talons extended, and lift a wriggling fish triumphantly aloft. Despite her apprehension about ever finding Mr. Joel Rivers, she felt a quickening of her heart as the bird soared higher with its prey. The beauty of this place was spellbinding.

The ferry dock, if four posts connected by numerous weathered planks could be called such, was just around the corner. A round little man was sitting on a barrel on the back of the ferry, tossing bread crumbs into the air to six screeching gulls. He looked up as Emma stopped her car but made no move to relinquish his seat.

"Excuse me," Emma said, getting out of her car. "I'm looking for Thorn Haven."

After a long pause, during which Emma wondered if the man was deaf, he stood up, pushed back his cap, and scratched his head thoughtfully. "Well now, honeychild," he said in a voice as scratchy as an old phonograph needle, "that car of yours got nary wings nor gills."

"I beg your pardon," Emma said hesitantly. Was his tractor missing a wheel? as Aunt Charlotte would say.

"The road to Thorn Haven be a mite damp." He gestured across the water and chuckled. "Out in Eastern Bay there."

"You mean . . . it's an *island?*" she asked in disbelief. Curse Sunny and her messy map. Emma had never trusted boats nor water, and an island was going to involve both.

Five minutes later Emma's car was secured on the ferry, which looked as though it were just waiting to be untied from the dock so it could sink like a rock. Emma sat on a dingy barrel in the pilothouse, the only object that could pass as a chair. *Oh, Lord* was about the only thought that kept surfacing in Emma's head. She made a mental vow to throttle Sunny if she lived through this.

The ferryman introduced himself as Hiram Bender and offered Emma the tin of sardines he'd just opened, but she politely declined. As the ferry edged away from the dock Hiram observed, "Fishing's been good for that there osprey." Emma dared a look out the window and saw the same bird she'd watched earlier now gliding over the water. "Brought two tourists back from Thorn Haven just this morning," Hiram said, chewing a sardine. "*They* didn't catch nothing. Should take a few lessons from the bird, I guess."

Emma felt the pitch of waves under the boat and decided to talk, hoping that it would take her mind off the fact that only a few planks stood between her and Davy Jones's locker. "Do people come to Thorn Haven to fish then?" she asked.

"As many as not," the cryptic Hiram said cheerfully. "We be what outsiders label 'quaint.' And we ain't all that pleased about the attention." He jerked his thumb behind him. "Town wanted to take down the ferry sign awhile back. We figure that if a person wants to get here bad enough he'll find the ferry. And if he ain't the patient sort, then we don't want him anyway." Another sardine slid down his throat, signalled by the bobbing of Hiram's Adam's apple. "Now I don't figure you for the fishing sort. You one of them perfessors, honeychild? They's always turning up to write down our stories and such."

Emma cleared her throat. "Well, no, not actually. I'm looking for Joel Rivers. He's . . . taking care of my nephew."

Hiram scratched his head and put his cap back on. "Rivers, huh? Well, there's as many Riverses on Thorn Haven as fish in the Bay. The rest be Taylors, Bakers—and Benders, like me." Off came the cap as he scratched his head again. "There's Joe and Joseph and Jody Rivers, all on the west side, and then there's Joel who crabs. Yeah, that would be Buckshot you want."

"Buckshot?" This was sounding less promising by the minute.

Hiram nodded. *"Eeyup,"* he drawled. "Folks hereabouts go by nickname, even in the phone book, to cut down the confusion. Like as I can recall, you'll find Buckshot in the tavern. Don't think he went out crabbin' today." As Emma digested this, Hiram gave a snort and pointed out the window. Emma could see the misty beginnings of Thorn Haven, seeming to emerge from the water itself. Other boats chugged toward the dock, and Emma could make out bushel baskets piled high on the decks.

"There be the crabbers comin' home," Hiram said. "Lordy, but it looks like they got a dandy haul of Jimmies today, honeychild. Used to do a bit of crabbin' myself and some arsterin' too. Arthritis got me stove up now, so I don't go out much."

He talked on about his days on the water, but Emma couldn't get her mind off whatever lay ahead. She steeled herself to meet the man on the phone, the Buckshot who had begun his day in a tavern and was known to have punched out a football coach. *Courage, Emma,* she cheered herself. *He probably doesn't punch out women.*

The tavern, a dingy wooden affair sandwiched between a

dry-goods store and a laundromat on the cobblestone street, was the Stormy Seas according to the neon sign above the open door. She could hear a juke box blaring rock music as she parked the car and got out into the noon heat. She hesitated in front of the window and frowned at the hand-lettered cardboard sign announcing a wet T-shirt contest that night. She wished she had changed from her pink cotton shorts and white knit top, but they had been comfortable for driving and now it was too late to change. So she took a deep breath, flexed her toes in her sandals and entered the dark interior of the Stormy Seas. It took her eyes a moment to adjust, and then she was aware of other eyes watching her. She looked around slowly and saw a table in a dark recess of the room and around it five men, glasses, and a pitcher of beer in front of them. They were grisly by Emma's mild standards, dressed in stained sweat shirts with the arms cut off, and grimy, torn jeans. They wore caps tilted back on their heads, and they were definitely giving her the once-over. She wondered which one was Joel Rivers. Probably the most repulsive of the lot.

Emma swung her eyes to the bar on the right where some kind of loud discussion was in progress over the juke box's noise. Three girls in cut-off jeans and tank tops were all talking at once and two men behind the bar were answering, and nobody could hear what anyone else was saying.

The darker of the two men behind the bar arrested Emma's attention, and she found herself staring at him. His wavy black hair set off a bronze tan along with eyes so starkly green that she could identify their color from across the room. He was tall and lean, and her eyes followed the movement of one tautly muscled arm as he raised a big hand to brush back his hair in agitation. He raised both hands in the air and scowled at the girls and then the man next to him. "All right, hold it!" he commanded, and almost instantly they all fell silent. "Juice, turn off that damn noise!"

Juice must have been the other bartender, because the intense young man with wide eyes and sandy hair hurried to do the job.

"Now, *ladies,*" the dark man said, turning those incredible eyes on the girls, "you may *not* wear bikini bottoms in the wet T-shirt contest. Cut-offs are as risqué as we're getting. Understand?" The girls grumbled in chorus but apparently accepted the man's decision. They turned and started for the doorway, and Emma saw when they got closer that each one was probably all of twenty-one. Oh, the good old days, Emma thought. If she were twenty-one instead of twenty-nine she might have entered the contest, too. No, she wouldn't. But Sunny would.

Their grievance apparently forgotten, the girls giggled as they passed Emma. "God, he's cute!" one moaned.

"Yeah, but he's old," another said, dousing the flames of young passion.

Emma had to agree with the cute, although it was a mild term for her own assessment. But, by her standards he certainly wasn't old. About thirty-five, she'd say.

He came around the bar, a towel slung over his shoulder, and stopped at a table to pick up some empty glasses. Emma found she couldn't take her eyes off him. His face was classically handsome with a square jaw shadowed by an afternoon's growth of beard. A firm, wide mouth deepened the grooves in the hollows of his cheekbones whenever he spoke. Dark brows and a straight nose gave a patrician cast to what otherwise would have been a rough-and-tumble, rugged handsomeness. His jeans did little to hide slim hips and muscular thighs, and the white shirt, sleeves rolled up, exposed a feathering of dark hair on his arms and clung tantalizingly to a steely chest. He looked like he should be a steelworker or a cowboy, not a bartender.

"Juice, don't forget to order some extra maraschino cherries," he called over his shoulder, still scowling. "We're almost out and all those tourists here tonight will be ordering drinks with more fruit than liquor."

"Yeah, yeah, sure," Juice called from behind the bar.

"I'll be glad when this damn contest is over," he muttered. He looked up then and caught Emma staring at him. She flushed, realizing what her face must register. His eyes were *so* green. And right now they were locked with her own blue ones. She felt her breath catch and quiver in her chest. The scowl momentarily eased, replaced by a flicker of searing interest. But then that fleeting expression quickly passed, and the frown was back. He walked slowly toward her. Emma could feel her heart pound with each step that brought him closer.

He stopped in front of her and let his eyes drop down over her knit top and shorts before he stared at the knit top again. She didn't know what he was doing when he reached out, but her breath caught as he adjusted her collar, which must have been turned up. Hard fingers grazed her neck, and Emma's pulse flicked to throbbing life beneath the touch. She could see surprise register on his face, as if his own reaction was as intense as hers and just as unexpected. His hand stayed a split second too long to be merely casual, and then he withdrew. She must be awfully tired, she reasoned with herself, to feel this impulsive, intense attraction for this man, especially now that his scowl was firmly back in place.

He took a step backward and glared at her again, making

Emma acutely uncomfortable. "That top . . ." He shook his head.

"What?" Emma said, startled.

"Look," he said with exaggerated patience. "That thing's far too lightweight and . . . revealing. You wear that in here, honey, and you're looking for more than just a drink."

Bingo! Emma's blood pressure soared into the stratosphere. Widowhood had not relegated Emma to an older generation, but everyone she knew except Sunny treated her as if she'd grown thirty years older the day Paul died. Emma found herself invited to work in the kitchen with the older women during church suppers, and then there were the store clerks who suggested she put that short skirt back and try on the pants suit instead. *It fits your image better, dear,* one Parton salesclerk told her. Emma didn't trust herself to ask what that image was, but she guessed she was the town's only post-marriage virgin. And now, here was this infuriating man insulting her clothes. Who the hell did he think he was, anyway!

"Look here yourself, *honey,*" she said indignantly. "I don't remember hiring you to supervise my wardrobe. And I'll thank you to keep your opinions to yourself."

She saw fire in those green eyes, but she was too angry to take much notice of the answering fire in her veins.

"I've had a rough morning, *lady,*" he retorted. "And that blouse of yours is my concern as long as you come in here wearing it. A few drops of water and you'll be showing more skin than a *Playboy* centerfold. Frankly, I've had it up to here with this wet T-shirt contest and all you pretty young things acting so eager to put your . . . *assets* on display for the entire male population."

"Hey, where's that new carton of swizzle sticks?" Juice hollered from the bar.

"How the hell should I know?!" Mr. Charm roared over his shoulder.

"Now, wait a minute here," Emma began.

His eyes came back to her and drifted over the knit top, spending more time than necessary on her breasts.

"We aren't out of them, are we?" Juice called back.

"Naw, I just saw that new box yesterday," he said. "Look in the storeroom. And check on those cherries while you're there."

"Excuse me," Emma tried again, this time with exaggerated politeness. He glanced back at her, scowling, and Emma noted with increasing irritation that his eyes lingered on the offending top. For heaven's sake! For someone who professed to find her top too skimpy, he was spending enough time staring at it.

"And wash some more beer glasses," he called over his shoulder in distraction. "We'll need plenty tonight."

"Will you listen to me!" Emma cried in annoyance. This time he gave her his full attention, though his jaw jutted at a stubborn angle and those green eyes dipped back below her neck. "First, you can just stop *looking* at me," she informed him, and he had the good grace to attempt to shift his eyes upward. "And second, you can try to get it through your thick skull that I'm not here for your silly T-shirt contest! I came in here looking for someone and you jump all over me about my clothes."

A puzzled expression, followed by chagrin, flitted over his face. "Hey, I'm sorry," he said, giving her an off-center smile as he rubbed the back of his neck in obvious embarrassment. "It's been a zoo in here all morning, and I've had my fill of giggly girls wanting to get maximum exposure in this damn contest."

"Well, I don't think much of your contest," Emma

sniffed, refusing to be mollified so easily by that charming smile.

"Yeah," he said, shrugging his shoulders. "Neither do I, but Juice and I don't own the bar. Listen, I'm sorry if I jumped to conclusions."

"Jumped?" Emma said with a lift of her brows. "I'd say you did warp speed."

He finally met her eyes, making her feel a strange combination of heat and chill. She couldn't stop looking at him. That crooked grin was back. "Well, let me see if I can do something right," he said. "Just who is it you're looking for? Maybe I can help."

"Mr. Joel Rivers."

"Buckshot?" he asked, a note of surprise in his voice. "That one?"

Emma nodded. "I need to find my nephew Cory."

The bartender looked taken aback. "I guess I can help you after all," he said slowly. "I'm the man you're looking for." Emma was momentarily speechless, trying to reconcile her mental picture of the telephone ogre with this man. He looked at her more closely. "Hey," he said suddenly. "You're not Aunt Emma, are you?"

She stared back in bewilderment. "But I thought you were . . . were some kind of fisherman."

"A crabber," he affirmed, and she saw some change coming over his face as he stared at her. Apparently he was remembering their phone conversation. "I tend bar part-time. It helps bring in some extra money, and since I've got to pay for my busted alternator today—I'm tending bar." He looked her over with wary interest. "So you're Aunt Emma," he said speculatively.

"We've already established that," Emma said testily, wishing he'd stop looking at her. "Now, where's Cory?"

"He's at camp all day. He'll be home tonight. One of the coaches drops him and Mike off when I can't pick them up. Hey—" He took her arm, and though Emma tried to wrest it away she wasn't successful. She couldn't seem to quell a rising response to his touch either. She felt as though some other woman was controlling her body. "Come on over here and sit down," he said, propelling her by her arm to a table. He called over his shoulder to Juice for two glasses of soda, and when he had her seated opposite him, she still felt the pressure of his absent fingers on her arm, like a caressing shadow.

Juice shot him a wide grin, accompanied by a raise of bushy eyebrows as he set the glasses down, and Emma flushed, knowing she was the object of the look.

"Don't you have glasses to wash?" Rivers said pointedly, and Juice finally shuffled off, throwing another grin over his shoulder.

"Mr. Rivers," Emma said stiffly, determined to ignore his effect on her. She concentrated on her glass, refusing to look at his face. "I'm worried about Cory."

"He's all right," he assured her. "He's really enjoying the camp, and he and Mike have become good friends."

"But this stealing . . ."

"It hasn't been repeated. He seems happy where he is now."

"Which is at your house," Emma said, frowning. "I'm going to take him home with me."

"I don't think that would be a good idea," he said, and she made the mistake of looking across the table at him. He was leaning back on two chair legs, watching her, his face dark and unfathomable. "Cory needs some stability right now."

"He has a family and stability in Iowa," Emma retorted,

intrigued despite her anger by that haunted look in his eyes.

"From what I understand there's a new baby at his house, and his mother was recently divorced. His father moved out of state to remarry."

Emma flushed angrily. His information was accurate and delivered in a cold, no-punches-pulled tone. And she heard the implication behind his words. She and Sunny were neglecting Cory. All right, she admitted wearily. Maybe Sunny was too involved in the baby and in salving her divorce-torn emotions to give Cory all the time he needed. And Emma was always snowed under at the store. But Cory was loved, and he knew it.

"Dammit!" Emma snapped, pushed to swearing by his arrogance. This was none of his business! She snatched at her glass and spilled it as she was lifting it to her mouth. Tempted to swear again, she slammed the glass back on the table. There was soda on her arm, and she reached blindly for a napkin. Before she could get one, his chair thunked as he leaned forward. She felt a gentle stroking of her arm and saw that he had taken the towel from his shoulder and was drying her arm with it. Emma couldn't seem to move her arm away, and the stroking was like a flame licking at her raw nerves. *Go away,* Emma ordered the distinctly female sensations oozing from every crevice in her body, but the cravings just grew stronger. She was starkly aware of being a woman, and that awareness grew sharper with each touch of his hand on her arm. *Whatever you do, don't look in*

. . . his eyes. They were so green and so gentle and so *male.* And when they stared at her like this, unguarded, they stole her breath away. Her lips parted slightly, and she couldn't turn her gaze.

Abruptly the scowl returned to his face and he pulled his

hand from her arm. He leaned back, and the shadows in the bar fell across his eyes.

Quickly Emma stood up, knowing she would be tempting the Henley Family Curse if she stayed another second in this place with this man.

She frowned and forced her eyes to look past his shoulder. "I'm going to find a place to stay, Mr. Rivers," she said, surprised at the calmness in her voice. "And tonight I want to see Cory. If you'll tell me where the nearest hotel is, I'll check in and you can bring Cory by when he gets through with camp."

"I'm sorry, Ms.—" He stood up and stepped toward her.

"Emma Kendrick," she said coolly. At least he'd stopped calling her Aunt Emma.

"Ms. Kendrick, this is the tourist season, and the motel's filled. The boardinghouses, too."

"So what am I supposed to do?" Emma demanded as if this new detail was his fault.

He was silent a long moment, looking at her, and Emma focused on his shirt, which seemed the only safe place to look. At last he sighed and extracted a key ring from his pocket. Now what? Emma wondered. He took off one key and pushed it toward her hand until she took it. "What's this?" she said.

"The key to my house, Ms. Kendrick," he said dryly. "And remember, I've counted the silver."

She ignored his cute little wisecrack and shook her head. "Thank you, but no."

"It's either that or sleep in your car," he informed her. "I could probably get you in Mrs. Grundy's, but I don't have the time to go talk to her right now." His eyes challenged her, and she realized there didn't seem to be any choice.

"All right," she murmured stiffly.

"Follow this street out of town, then take a right on Old Hook Road. The house is a big white clapboard. Third on the left. The name's on the mailbox." And with that, he turned on his heel and headed toward Juice, already demanding to know if he'd checked on those cherries yet. *So that's that,* Emma thought as she stepped outside into the sunshine and heat.

She stared at the few houses and shops as she drove down the street, turning on Old Hook Road when she was well past the last house. But her mind wasn't on her driving. She was thinking of the man back in the bar. She got the distinct impression that, though he had offered her his house, he was anxious for her to be on her way. And it was just as well. Sea-green eyes or not, Emma wasn't risking the family curse.

She braked sharply when she almost drove past the house. It was practically invisible from the road, cloaked by a wind-wracked grove of pine trees. The drive wound through the trees, and Emma slowed down as the house came into view. It was recently painted, and the green shutters gleamed in the hot sun. It was a large, rambling house with two chimneys and was obviously very old. Some red geraniums, wilting, grew in the flowerbed next to the stone steps. Emma's attention was so focused on the house that she didn't realize there was anything in the drive until she heard the crunch. Hastily she braked and jumped out to inspect the damage. There were some chicken-wire cages strewn in the drive, and she had hit two of them. They were dented, but not entirely crushed. Emma decided they looked pretty useless anyway and probably weren't important.

She pulled the cages from under the car, then walked around to look at the house. Untended flowerbeds lay baking in the sun with an occasional dragonfly rising from a weed to dart away. The lawn behind the house, sparsely covered in coarse, dry grass, sloped away to the flat, blue, glassy surface of the Eastern Bay, a section of the Chesapeake from what she had been able to ascertain from Sunny's map. Water slapped playfully at the stones along the edge of the yard. There was a clothesline back there, too, and more trees. Bumblebees droned sonorously in a wild vine that had draped itself around a large cherry tree. Emma swatted at a small fly that landed on her arm and bit her, then walked back to the front of the house. A johnboat lay bottom up in the grass, as though time and tide had washed it there. A calico cat hurried down the porch steps and mewed an urgent message as it ran to Emma. She bent down and stroked its back as the cat purred in pleasure and leaned against her leg, swishing its tail.

"Are you the welcoming committee?" Emma murmured, giving the cat one last pat before standing up again. They walked up the steps together, the cat impatiently weaving in and out between Emma's legs as she tried the key in the lock. When the door opened, the cat breezed in first and headed straight for a big stuffed chair by the massive stone fireplace. The house was cool, and a hint of a breeze drifted in through an open window. Emma wondered why Joel Rivers bothered to lock his door when almost every window in the house was open. A fly buzzed past her head and apparently dive-bombed the cat, which twitched an ear and blinked solemnly.

Emma was exhausted, not even possessing enough energy to hunt for the bathroom or the bedroom. The couch looked just fine. She pushed aside a rumpled newspaper and stretched out. She was just closing her eyes when she heard the soft plop of paws hitting the floor. An instant later the cat joined Emma on the couch and curled up contentedly by her chin. Emma fell asleep to the sound of purring.

Emma wasn't sure later what woke her first, the light coming on or the sound of swearing. She didn't know where she was at first, and she sat up quickly, making the cat hustle down to the relative safety of the couch arm. She stared around and slowly realized it was Joel Rivers' living room. She must have slept for hours. It was dark outside, and the ceiling light was on.

An expletive came from the next room, then a light came on there. Emma blinked and frowned. What was going on here? If this was a burglary, then that was one testy burglar.

"Two weeks work!" came the angry mutter from the kitchen. Footsteps thudded on the floor, and Emma stared as Joel Rivers stepped into the living room and caught sight of her. He frowned and looked as though he'd found her ransacking his silver chest after all. "What are you doing here?" he demanded.

Emma's surprise evaporated into irritation. "*You* gave me your house key, remember?"

"Yeah, I know," he said impatiently. "But I thought you'd pick a bed to sack out on." His eyes dropped to the cat regarding him with wide-eyed placidity. "What did you do, give Charles a tranquilizer?"

Emma stroked the cat—*Charles*. "He didn't seem to need one," she said coolly. "Unlike some people."

He frowned again and looked at her, then at the cat with equal annoyance. He certainly seemed at a loss for words for someone who had fired off several interesting epithets in the kitchen a moment ago.

"Is there some problem with my sleeping on the couch?"

Emma asked, meeting his eyes boldly and then quickly looking away when her boldness threatened to dissolve into something else.

He shook his head. "No," he growled.

"Then what is the problem?"

"Ms. Kendrick," he said with exaggerated patience, putting his hands on his hips. "Do you always make it a practice to run over anything in your path or are you just nearsighted?"

Emma frowned and tried to think what on earth he was talking about. Casting back, she vaguely remembered hitting something as she pulled into the drive. "The chicken-wire things?" she guessed.

"*Chicken-wire things?*" he said with barely controlled irritation. "Those were crab pots."

Emma still didn't see the significance. "Surely they can't be that valuable."

A vein was throbbing in his temple. "Ms. Kendrick," he said from between clenched teeth, "crab pots are not chicken wire. They are made of steel wire treated with zinc, and they cost more than anything you'll find in a hen house."

"Oh. I'm sorry." She truly felt bad about hitting the crab pots, whatever they were used for, but he didn't seem particularly interested in the pots anymore. His eyes had strayed to her legs, and Emma tried to summon a proper amount of indignation. Instead, she felt a warm flush spreading upward from her bare toes, a flush that became an insistent tingle when it reached her stomach. Oh my word, she groaned inwardly. The Henley Family Curse was rearing its ugly head again—she was definitely attracted to this arrogant bartender/fisherman/crab-pot enthusiast. Well, heaven help us all, she warned herself, standing up. She tucked in her top, aware of his eyes roaming upward to the flash of bare stomach briefly showing.

Emma forced her toes to relax and stop curling upward, then made herself look into his eyes. "Mr. Rivers, I will pay for your crab crocks—"

"Pots."

"Whatever." His mouth was so firm and inviting . . . She broke off her distracting inventory of his handsome face and went on. "Just prepare a bill, including your expenses for Cory, and I'll take care of it tomorrow. Then Cory and I will head home."

"Prepare a bill?" he repeated in disbelief. "Is that how you and your sister amble through life, Ms. Kendrick? Just give me the bill and I'll be on my way?"

Emma was livid, but before she could fire off a retort, he abruptly turned and left the room.

She wondered if he was out in the kitchen slamming his fist into something. Emma sighed, listening to the sounds of the refrigerator opening and closing. No doubt his son was a real pistol, too. For the first time, she wondered where the boy's mother was.

Joel Rivers came back to the living room, still glowering, and thrust one of two cans of beer at Emma. "Drink this, Kendrick," he ordered in a throaty growl.

"No, thank you," she said stiffly.

"Kendrick, I know what you need," he said, pushing the beer into her hand until she was forced to hold it.

"I sincerely doubt that," Emma said with raised brows.

"Look, I've had a rough day," he said irritably.

"And that's my fault?" Emma retorted.

Before he could answer a car door slammed and then the back door opened. "Hey! We're home!" The voice was cheerful, and Emma could hear footsteps coupled with a shuffling gait.

Cory and another boy appeared in the kitchen doorway, and Emma quickly glanced at Joel Rivers, trying to overcome her shock at the sight of his son. He was watching her, and Emma realized in that instant that her reaction was very important, not only to the boy, but to his father as well.

Cory was staring in astonishment. "Em! What are you doing here?"

Emma walked to the boys, smiling. "I came to fetch you home, urchin," she said, ruffling Cory's hair. "And you must be Mike. It's a pleasure to meet a good friend of Cory's." She extended her hand. Mike's thin, lanky legs were encased in long metal braces attached to a pelvic band at the top and a bar between heavy shoes at the bottom. He leaned on metal crutches that circled his wrists. He looked surprised momentarily, and then he smiled shyly and shook her hand.

"You can't take me home!" Cory wailed, astonishment turning rapidly to distress. "Camp's not over. You can't, Em!"

She looked to Joel Rivers and saw from the relaxed set of his jaw that she'd done the right thing with his son. Apparently that carried a lot of weight, because he came to her rescue. "Why don't we talk about it in the morning? You guys had a long day, and so did Ms. Kendrick."

"We don't have to go to bed already, do we?" Mike pleaded.

"I'm afraid so, cowboy," his father said, and Emma couldn't help noticing the warmth in Rivers' voice and eyes. "You two go get cleaned up and I'll be in to say good night in a little bit." He took a look at the crestfallen faces in front of him and sighed. "I think Mrs. Gamble might have left some cupcakes in the kitchen if you two are hungry."

"Oh, wow, yeah," Cory enthused, and both boys headed back to the kitchen, Mike's slower shuffle trailing after Cory.

"Drink a glass of milk, too," Rivers advised in a loud voice.

Emma was wrestling with a dozen questions when he turned back to her, not the least of which was, What was a boy in braces doing in a football camp?

Rivers smiled and shrugged. "Why don't I put some clean sheets on the guest bed?" His face took on a whole new aspect when he smiled, and Emma found herself staring again.

She shook her head dubiously. "I just don't think that would work . . ."

"Well, there's always Mrs. Grundy's," he said, and the smile broadened.

CHAPTER THREE

Now what was going on over there? Emma mused as she stared out the window of her room at Mrs. Grundy's. The bedroom was on the third floor of a nineteenth-century stone house across the road from Rivers' house. From this height Emma could see the Rivers house, and now, at 3 a.m., she saw that lights were on in the ground-level rooms and a new car was parked in the drive.

Joel Rivers had had a hard time controlling his mirth as he took Emma and her suitcase across the road to Mrs. Grundy's the night before. Emma had had the presence of mind to leave her can of beer on his coffee table, and she was grateful for that foresight when Mrs. Grundy's steely eyes studied her critically.

"Well, I suppose she could rent the room on the top floor," she'd grudgingly allowed when her inspection ended. "Doesn't drink, does she?"

A throaty sound emerged from Joel Rivers. "Only on social occasions," he said gravely.

Emma glared at him. "Well, just make sure no social occasions come up while you're here," Mrs. Grundy warned Emma. "No cooking in the kitchen after seven, and you have to wash your own dishes. This way." The glances Rivers threw her way as they climbed the stairs behind Mrs. Grundy let her know just how cute he thought this whole situation was. "Now remember," he reminded her in an undertone as he deposited her suitcase inside the spacious bedroom, "don't booze it up."

Emma gave him a telling look, and he chuckled as he turned to go back down the steps.

Emma wondered what the heck he was up to now. Certainly he didn't have to tend bar at three in the morning. She hadn't been able to sleep because of the long nap she'd had at his house, but he had been working and shouldn't be suffering from insomnia.

Well, she might as well walk to his house and get her car now, she decided, rather than wait for him to bring it over later as he'd promised. Her small makeup case was behind the front seat, and she didn't even have a toothbrush here in her room.

The stairs creaked as Emma descended in her jeans, pink cotton blouse, and sneakers, and she saw the bedroom door on the second floor open a crack. No doubt Mrs. Grundy thought she was about to use the kitchen at an illegal hour.

The morning was damp and chilly, and Emma rubbed her upper arms briskly as she hurried across the road. She was just starting up the drive when his blue pickup with its camper shell came toward her, its lights burning through the dusky mist. He apparently didn't see her and didn't slow down, so Emma waved her arms over her head.

The pickup skidded to a halt next to her, and he leaned over to roll down the passenger window. "What are you trying to do, get run over?" he demanded.

"It seemed the perfect way to start the day," Emma assured him, "especially after yesterday was such a winner." She opened the door and climbed in.

"Hey, what are you doing?"

"We have to talk, and since you seldom stand still for more than five minutes at a time and you sleep even less, I'm coming with you."

He sighed in exasperation. "You can't do that."

Emma couldn't help noticing how his dark hair fell carelessly across his forehead. He was wearing a blue Windbreaker which accentuated his green eyes, and he looked darn good. But Emma was determined not to be deterred from her mission. He was probably just going out for breakfast anyway. "Unless you're going to a stag party at this hour, I'm coming with you," she said decisively.

He set his jaw and jammed the truck into gear. They took off with the force of a rocket, and Emma was thrown hard against him as he swung the truck onto the road. She straightened up as soon as she regained her equilibrium, but not before she got a whiff of clean soap and the feel of hard muscles beneath the Windbreaker. "Mission Control, we have a launch," she said dryly.

His jaw clenched tighter, and they rode in silence for five more minutes, Emma gripping the armrest in self-defense.

"Did you leave someone with the boys?" she asked, thinking of the new car in the drive.

"Mrs. Gamble, the housekeeper. She keeps everyone in line."

"Mrs. Grundy's sister, no doubt," Emma commented, and that at least drew a reluctant smile from him.

The lines in his face softened when he smiled, and he looked years younger. Emma felt her heart contract, and she turned her head to look out the window. They were turning toward the dock.

"Okay, Kendrick, we're here," he said, parking the truck and shutting off the engine.

"This is the dock," she said.

"Good," he praised her sarcastically. "You're beginning to recognize landmarks."

She was too worried to take exception to his flippant tone. "You're not going fishing, are you?"

"You learn fast, Ms. Kendrick," he said. "I drive to the dock, I'm carrying crab pots, therefore I'm going fishing."

"But I need to talk to you," she said anxiously, scanning the place for someone who could drive her back to the house. She had to settle this thing about Cory.

"Then you'll have to come with me," he told her flatly.

"But, I . . ." she began, and then cleared her throat. "Actually I'm afraid of the water."

"What?" he said in mock surprise, a smile teasing his mouth. "A strong, independent Iowa woman like yourself. Kendrick! Don't they have water in Iowa?"

"Of course they have water," she snapped. "Large bodies of water like the Mississippi, but I don't make a practice of going too near them."

He leaned back against the truck seat and sighed. "Would it help if you wore a life vest and had a railing to hold onto?"

He was serious, and she was grateful he wasn't making fun of her. "I suppose so," she said in a small voice.

"Okay. Then let's go." He got out of the truck and shut the door, while Emma continued to sit inside the truck uncertainly. She could still turn back, she reasoned. It wasn't too late. She could just pack up Cory and head for home and forget about Joel Rivers.

He stopped and turned to look at her. "Come on, Kendrick," he said. "Stop dilly-dallying or you're going to miss a great sunrise."

She'd miss a lot of great sunrises if she died of fright in the middle of the Chesapeake Bay, she thought, but something made her get out of the truck and follow him. He was getting a cooler and one of those chicken-wire—correction, steel wire—things out of the back of the truck's camper shell. He gave her a long look as he started toward the boats

40

and motioned with his head. Emma fell into step beside him, noticing despite her increasing dread of this excursion how his arm muscles strained against his Windbreaker. He told her to wait beside a piling, assuring her she could hold onto it if she'd feel better, and then he was marching back to the truck. Emma stared down at the cooler instead of at the boats, and hugged her arms. It was still chilly, and only a faint smudge of gray showed on the black horizon. Hearing the water slap rhythmically against the moored boats, Emma was tempted to grab the piling and hold on for dear life, but the memory of the glint in Rivers' eyes kept her from doing it.

"All set," he said beside her, making her jump as he laid two more wire cages on the wooden planks. Around them, farther down the dock, shadowy figures got out of trucks and moved silently and swiftly, loading boats and boarding. A motor chugged to life in the distance.

Emma looked up and realized that he was watching her, and that made her stomach twist strangely. There was no denying he was a compelling, handsome man. And Emma was not immune to that.

"That's my boat over there," he said, his eyes not leaving her face as he pointed down the dock. Emma looked that way and then glanced at him in confusion. "This is a friend's boat," he said, picking up a crab pot and hoisting it on board. "Dave came down with a case of something or other—" The way he said it made Emma guess that the illness was either imagined or somehow reprehensible. "—and I told him I'd do his crab pots today." He glanced over his shoulder. "He has a seven-year-old son." The weight given those words convinced Emma the son was the reason Joel Rivers was doing Dave's crab pots.

He helped her on board and when his callused fingers

closed around her arm Emma felt the blood gather there. The boat seemed to be rocking violently or maybe it was only her imagination. "Sit there," he ordered, pointing her toward a thin wooden bench in front of a small cabin near the front of the boat. "And put this on." He reached into a chest at the side of the boat and handed her a life vest.

Emma dared a glance around as he finished the loading. She knew nothing about boats, but this one seemed immense in comparison to the little rowboat her father sometimes used for fishing. It was maybe thirty-five feet in length and loaded with a baffling array of things she didn't understand. There were at least a dozen wooden barrels, an equal number of bushel baskets, a big garbage container, and six small baskets that smelled fishy. Emma glanced over her shoulder into the window of the little cabin. She could see a radio on a shelf and a bunch of papers and empty coffee cups. A small single bed was built into the wall.

He came up behind her while she was conducting her visual survey, and his voice startled her. "If you're looking for a seat belt, I'm afraid you're out of luck." She turned around, noticing that he was grinning and looking all too pleased with himself. The grin was doing strange things to her balance that had nothing to do with the rocking of the boat, and she found to her consternation that she sort of liked it.

"I thought maybe I should write my will," she retorted dryly.

"Ah, poor suspicious Ms. Kendrick," he said with mock sympathy. "You have nothing to worry about. Once we get out on the water you'll be too busy to be scared."

"Busy?"

"Very," he said, and with no further explanation he pulled a green cap from his pocket, jammed it on his head, and began easing the boat away from the dock.

Twenty minutes later he stopped the boat, and they sat in the enveloping misty shroud of night's end. Emma had no idea where they were or how Rivers had found his way. He pulled a thermos from the cooler and poured two cups of coffee. "Here," he said, handing her one of the Styrofoam cups. Then he frowned. "Why didn't you tell me you were cold?"

She hadn't realized she was shivering until now. He stripped off his Windbreaker and handed it to her. "Here, put this on."

"But you—"

"I'm fine," he interrupted smoothly. "And drink the coffee."

He was pushy, she thought resentfully as she put on the jacket over her life vest. It bore a faint masculine smell and traces of his body warmth, and she found her blood warming in response. He sat down beside her and gave her a nudge with his arm. "You take up a lot of sitting room, Kendrick."

"Oh, thank you very much," she said. "Your coffee tastes like mud."

"I work hard to make it taste like that," he assured her. "You just don't have appreciative tastebuds."

"What are we sitting here waiting for?" she said. "For you to get tired of giving me a hard time?"

"We're waiting for sunrise, Kendrick. And when I give you a hard time you're not scared."

He was staring straight ahead, his forearms propped on his knees as he leaned forward, and Emma was struck again by how physically attractive he was. And he was right—she wasn't scared when she was arguing with him.

"Well," she said, partly mollified, "if you have a good reason."

He didn't look at her, but he was smiling again. And when he was smiling like that, that *No Intruders Allowed* attitude of his was temporarily gone. He shifted back until he was leaning against the wall, and they sat in a comfortable silence.

"Rivers?" Emma said at last.

"What is it, Kendrick?"

"Do you have . . . a wife somewhere?" she finally asked awkwardly.

"Rest assured," he said dryly. "I'm divorced."

She wondered where his ex-wife was, but she decided she'd asked enough nosy questions. There was a sting in the way he'd said divorced. She closed her eyes, lulled despite her fear by the gentle rocking of the boat.

An elbow in her ribs made her sit up abruptly and snap her eyes open. "What?" she complained.

"Geez, you're testy in the morning," he fumed. "Now focus your baby blues on that, Kendrick. That is a sunrise."

She followed his pointing finger to the skyline, and her breath caught in her throat. The palest hues of lavender, yellow, and pink glowed softly from the horizon, spreading their tints to everything around them—clouds, water, and even the gossamer mist rising from the Bay. As the light extended pastel fingers to stroke color into each cloud in the sky, Emma made out the faint black outline of trees on a distant shore. Mist floated in front of them like a sheen of silk, and Emma felt as though she were seeing the earth's first dawn. "It's beautiful," she murmured.

"I never get tired of it," he said, and Emma thought she understood how much he loved the Chesapeake by the timbre of his voice. Adrenaline coursed through her; part of it was the sunrise, the rest the presence of this man beside her.

"All right," he said, standing up. "Let's find Dave's markers."

Emma stared over the side, figuring she was fairly safe if she didn't relinquish her iron grip on the edge. A flash of red came into view, and Rivers slowed the boat. It was a buoy, and he idled the engine. Reaching into the chest, he pulled out two bright yellow things and tossed one to her, grinning.

Emma stared at the oilskin apron in her hands, then watched Rivers put his on. Dumbly she followed suit—thinking that if she fell overboard now in this heavy outfit nobody would find her before she washed out to sea. "Tie me," he ordered, turning around, and Emma fumbled with the strings in the back. He faced her again and ran critical eyes over her, clucking as he reached behind her to tie her apron. It was definitely nice standing here with his arms around her. His breath was warm in her hair as he leaned over to see what he was doing. *Very nice.* "Great caboose, Kendrick," he said.

"I thought it took up too much sitting room," she shot back, and he raised his eyebrows teasingly.

"Here." He stood back and handed her a pair of yellow gloves and she struggled into them, warming under his gaze. "Well, it's not high fashion," he said when she'd finished, "and you're damn well lost in that outfit, but you do look kind of cute." That was apparently to be the extent of his praise, because he turned away and busied himself with the boat. Emma sighed and looked down at herself. The apron nearly brushed the floor, and the gloves threatened to fall off if she straightened her fingers. She had to content herself with being called "cute."

He kicked a metal washtub until it rested in front of him, then nudged the boat forward, using the tiller to steer. He controlled the speed of the boat with knee pressure against the throttle. Emma saw two flanged wheels on the side of the boat, powered by a separate engine. Rivers reached over the side with some kind of long gaffing stick and pulled up a length of cord which he looped over the wheels. A second later up came one of the crab pots, and Emma watched in fascination. Streaming water, weeds, and junk, the pot nevertheless was filled with crabs.

He hoisted it aboard and rested it on a nearby ledge. Deftly he unsnapped a hook on the top of the pot, then tipped it sideways and opened a little box in the bottom. He shook out what must be old bait from the looks of it. Then he pressed open the seam on top of the pot and turned it upside down over the washtub, shaking. About thirty-five crabs tumbled out with a clatter. In fluid motion, Rivers reached into the barrel Emma'd noticed earlier and pulled out two handfuls of fish, stuffing them into the bait box. "Alewives," he told her over his shoulder. "Also called menhaden." He turned the whole affair right side up again and, glancing back at the last marker, tossed the pot overboard. "Okay," he said, idling the engine. "Now here's where I teach you to cull. And listen up. I don't want to get arrested for keeping crabs under the limit."

"Oh, God," Emma whispered under her breath.

"First you have to tell the sooks from the Jimmies," he said, and Emma stared at him blankly. He reached into the basin and pulled out a crab which proceeded to wave its claws menacingly in the air. Rivers turned it over on its back and showed Emma what he called the apron. "If it's shaped like an inverted T then that's a Jimmy, or male. If it's bell-shaped—" He reached into the basin and produced another crab. "—then it's a sook, or female. You'll also run into peelers which are crabs about to molt, but I'll have to help you with those." He showed her the notched stick for measuring from spine to spine across the crab and told her which barrels which crabs went into. "Okay?" he said, and before she could answer he was turning back to the engine, nudging the boat along toward the next marker.

Emma stared down at the mass of crabs and swallowed. She looked back at Rivers, but he was humming and staring out at the water. Apparently he wasn't going to be much help. She gathered her courage and stuck a gloved hand into the basin, coming up with a crab which promptly did its best to close a claw on her finger.

She managed to determine the sex—a Jimmy—and the size, and get the crab into the appropriate barrel. It seemed to her that she'd accomplished a lot, plucking out one crab and directing him to the right place, but Rivers was hauling in another pot, this one also loaded with crabs. Emma groaned in dismay as he turned around and raised his brows at her while he efficiently refilled the bait box.

The engine sputtered and nearly died, and Rivers frowned as he nudged the throttle. He came back to Emma and began helping her cull, and she was amazed at the speed at which he worked. "This crab's going to peel," he told her, indicating the color of part of one leg. "Probably in less than two weeks." That one went in a separate basket, although privately Emma noted that she'd seen no difference in color. It seemed there was some art to this after all.

Once again the engine sputtered, and he cursed under his breath. "Dave told me he was going to get this thing overhauled," he said, glowering. "Three times now someone's had to tow him in because of engine trouble."

"Is Dave always this careless?" Emma asked, frowning over a Jimmy as she measured him.

There was a short silence, then Rivers said quietly, "Yeah,

I'd say so." There was a lot more to it than those few words, and Emma threw him a sideways glance. There were layers to this man she was sure she'd never penetrate. Not that she'd be around long enough to anyway. As soon as she got rested up she planned to convince Cory that his mother needed him at home. Camp would always be here next year.

Cory. Emma frowned as she thought of him. She glanced at Rivers and then back down to the crabs. "Was Cory really stealing, Mr. Rivers?" she asked. "Or was it just some mistake?"

He didn't say anything, and when she dared a look at his face he was watching her thoughtfully. A dull ache began in her loins.

"He was caught red-handed," he said quietly. "He'd taken a couple of candy bars from a grocery store and stuck them in his pocket."

"But he knows better than that," Emma protested.

Rivers' eyes roved over her face, and she saw a softening of his features. "Ten-year-old boys often do things when they know better," he said.

"But Cory's never done anything like that before," she protested.

He was silent a moment, and his hands stilled. "He's just a little boy, Ms. Kendrick, and I think it's hard for him to understand what's happening in his family. With his dad going away."

Emma sighed. It was hard for everyone to understand. "Cory's father left . . . well, to marry another woman. None of us wanted to make Cory think poorly of his dad, so we haven't said much at all."

Rivers nodded. "He seems to think that it was somehow his fault. And now he sees being sent away to camp as a kind of banishment."

"Oh, no," Emma murmured, stricken.

"I think he was pretty miserable when he first got here. But he and Mike became friends, and Mike started bringing him home. Cory just seems to want someone to pay attention to him. I think that's why he stole those candy bars. Bad attention was better than none at all."

"And the camp expelled him?" Emma asked.

Rivers nodded. "It didn't strike me as a good way to help him, so I told the camp I'd be responsible for his behavior and he came to stay with Mike and me." He looked away from her face, pretending to be busy sorting crabs.

Emma cleared her throat. "That's very nice of you to take him in." She was more intrigued than ever by this man. "It must be difficult without a woman around . . . I mean . . ." She trailed off lamely.

"We manage," he said gruffly, and when he glanced at her face she saw such pride and pain in his eyes that she wanted to touch him and somehow make the pain go away.

She started to say something, anything, but she yelped instead. She looked down and saw a crab with one claw locked on her finger. Emma nearly swore in her distress and moved to stand up when Rivers quickly came to her rescue. He removed the crab and then made her take off her glove. "Hold still," he said in a gentle voice, inspecting her finger. He had pulled off his gloves and now his hand held hers, his fingers uncurling her own. Her pain faded as his touch pervaded her entire being. She looked at his face as his fingers lingered on hers and his eyes met hers, only inches away, green and blue locking like sea and sky on the horizon. No words passed between them, but the message was as clear as a front-page headline. He wanted her, too, and the thought made her exult even as her heart dropped. What was she getting herself into?

He stood up abruptly, frowning, and fetched something from a box in the little cabin. Emma watched his face through the window, seeing the signs of withdrawal. She was suddenly as cold as the emerald ice in his eyes.

He came back and bent over her again, this time with some gauze and disinfectant. The liquid stung for a moment, but Emma hardly felt that. She couldn't stop searching his face for some of the need she'd seen just a moment before. She felt his fingers brushing hers as he worked quickly and efficiently, but his touch was as impersonal as those eyes. Joel Rivers was determined not to need any woman, it seemed.

He taped a layer of gauze around her finger and stood up. "Let's get working," he said brusquely. "I have to replace some of these pots, and it's going to be a long day."

He wouldn't look at her again, and Emma turned back to the culling with stony determination.

They worked hard all morning, until Emma's back and shoulders ached with strain and fatigue. She was determined to keep up with the culling but it was impossible, and he had to help her with each new load. He didn't speak, and the early morning banter was a fading memory. She had stripped off his Windbreaker as the sun rose, and now a sheen of perspiration covered her face and arms. A cool breeze sprang up about nine and dark clouds began gathering in the west. Rivers kept glancing at them worriedly.

"Some thunderstorms and high winds were predicted for later today," he said tersely. "It's moving in early."

The fact that he'd even spoken to her let Emma know how serious he considered the storm. She went back to culling, but every now and then she cast a quick glance at the darkening sky.

"We'd better head for some shelter," he said at last,

throwing a pot over the side and hastily finishing the culling. "That front's moving pretty fast." The engine, which had coughed in sporadic shudders all morning, faltered again, and Rivers' jaw tightened.

The temperature was dropping by the second, and Emma slid into his Windbreaker again. Wind began to lash the boat with choppy waves, and the sky turned an ominous, eerie gray, a foreboding pallor that was nothing like the twilight that had heralded the sunrise that morning.

Five minutes later the rain hit. It didn't begin with gentle drops but a torrent of stinging needles of ice-cold water and hail. "Get in the cabin!" he yelled at her. He was working over the engine, pushing the boat forward into the teeth of the wind, then easing off when the engine complained. His cap had blown off and lay at his feet in a sodden pool of moisture. His dark hair was streaming water, and he paused occasionally to swipe at his face with the back of his arm.

Emma's teeth were chattering, but it was from fright rather than the cold. She glanced again at the low-hanging clouds, trailing down to the water like black veils. She felt too paralyzed to move. He looked at her again, and she saw the unspoken anxiety in his eyes. Calmly and deliberately he left the engine and came to her. "It's all right," he said quietly. "It's going to be all right." His arm around her shoulders, he led her to the cabin and made her sit on the small bed. He tipped up her chin and made her look him in the eyes, holding her gaze. "Don't worry," he ordered her. "I won't let anything happen to you."

Somehow she believed him, and she clung to that belief as he went back to the engine, his step quick and urgent. She could see the sky through the window, and it grew darker by the moment.

The boat pitched violently, and Emma was thrown

against the wall, banging her head. She righted herself and looked out of the window again, barely able to see through the sheets of rain. She blinked and stared again, sheer terror washing over her. A black funnel of swirling water and debris stretched between the waves and the heavens and it was coming straight for them.

The only coherent thought in Emma's head was how beautiful her last sunrise had been.

CHAPTER FOUR

It was dark and damp and something was thumping her head rhythmically. Emma gradually gained consciousness, and then, with her head throbbing so much she wanted to whimper, she let herself sink back to a semi-wakefulness.

In her groggy state she decided she must be back in the hospital. Now why did Dad let them admit me again? she wondered in annoyance. The hospital kept the curtains closed so that the room was dark, and that one nurse's aide was always bumping Emma's head with her elbow while she tried to rearrange the pillow. All that had changed the morning Dr. Lorilee Morgan marched into the room. She sat on the edge of Emma's bed and looked her in the eyes, hard. "Now why are you here?" she demanded.

"I couldn't stop crying," Emma said.

"And why not?"

"Because my husband died," Emma answered reasonably.

"I understand that was some time ago."

"Well, I didn't have any time to cry for the last six months," Emma said, remembering in a daze the long hours of endless work. "And then I just started crying."

"Ah," Dr. Morgan said, just the way Emma had heard psychologists murmur *ah* on TV. "You can't treat grief like a charge card, Mrs. Kendrick, running up the bill and putting off payment. One day it comes due." She had smiled at Emma then. "But I'm here to help you get through the grief." And so she had . . .

So why was she back in the hospital? That thumping was about to drive her crazy. Irritably Emma tried to push away the nurse's arm and instead made contact with heavy cloth. The grogginess drained away as she remembered what had happened. For a terrifying moment she was afraid she was under water and she sat up and thrashed until the fabric slid to her shoulders. Immediately rain pelted her hair and face and she stared around wildly, disoriented. She was on the ground next to a scruffy loblolly pine that shook and swayed in the blowing rain like a bedraggled kite tail. There was nothing else resembling shelter in the vicinity, she saw. The ground was flat and marshy, sandy here, although there were bent cattails and grass farther away. She looked around the other way and saw the shore, dotted in places by rocks. The wind slackened a second, just to catch its breath it seemed, and she could see the boat bobbing up and down offshore a bit. The sight made her head pound harder. The cabin roof was gone and the walls splintered. The glass had blown out of every window, and in the side of the boat itself was a gaping hole. *Joel Rivers!* My God, what if he was . . . ? *Dead.* Her heart plummeted to her feet.

"Hey! Get back under that tarp! Do you want pneumonia?"

She jumped and stared behind her, all panic evaporating as she saw him come limping from behind a rock, a load of wood in his arms.

"You crazy woman," he muttered as the wind began flailing her with rain again. He dumped the wood on the ground and turned to glare at her. "I said get under the tarp."

"Well, excuse me," she retorted around her clenched teeth. "I just poked my head out to see if I was dead or alive. And if that . . . that *thing* was coming back."

"Thank you kindly, Ms. Kendrick," he said sarcastically. "It's nice to know you were looking forward to my return."

"Not you," she told him, "that thing on the water that hit us. What are you doing!" she yelped as he dropped to the ground and began pulling her close to him. "Rivers!"

He didn't answer, just continued arranging her to suit himself until they were huddled together, her back against his chest, the tarp over them tent-style. "Well, you *sound* okay," he noted in the darkness of their cocoon.

"Listen, give me a minute here," she said, "and I'll give you a dissertation on how un-okay I am. *What* are you doing? Ow!" She was trying unsuccessfully to push his hands away from her head where he was probing.

"Hold still," he said. "I was worried about this bump on the head you got, especially when I saw you sitting there with rain pouring down your face. I mean, the accident could have made you more addled."

"More addled?" she repeated in irritation.

"Just testing," he assured her, and she felt him smile against her hair.

His nearness was robbing her of all reason, and to divert herself she asked, "What was that thing that hit the boat?"

"That was a waterspout."

"No kidding," she said dryly. "It felt like a freight train."

"A waterspout, Kendrick," he said patiently, "is a tornado on water. You have tornadoes in Iowa, don't you?"

"Of course. I know tornadoes. I just never saw one go after a boat before. It was like that movie about that huge shark."

He laughed then, and Emma felt warm as his chest moved against her. Apparently he was finished poking her head. She shifted slightly in the dark under the tarp, bringing her hand to his outstretched leg for balance, and she felt him flinch.

"What is it?" she demanded, twisting around to search his face in the darkness.

"It's nothing," he said. "Just a leg cramp." He might have been a convincing liar with someone else but not with Emma Kendrick. Her dark journey into grief had wrought changes in her, sometimes unwelcome ones. And since that time in the past when she had started crying and couldn't stop, Emma could hear the pain in other people's voices, be it physical or mental. And she heard pain in Joel Rivers' deep timbre.

"You're hurt," she insisted. "Where? Your leg?" She was trying to turn around all the way so she could see him properly, or at least as properly as she could in this darkness, but he seemed determined to hold her where she was, which was against his chest, his arms locked around her. "Will you *please* let go of me," she demanded breathlessly, her lack of air more than a little connected with the close contact of that solid chest and those strong arms holding her.

"We have to keep warm, Kendrick," he grumbled.

"We can keep warm after I find out where you're hurt," she assured him. "Now be reasonable."

He let her wriggle out of his embrace this time, and she turned around, kneeling on her knees, careful not to bump him. "Shall I light a match?" he asked sarcastically.

"Shhhhh!" She frowned over his leg, lifting just the corner of the tarp to let in a little light. His left leg was folded under him, so it must be all right. But the right one was stretched out straight in front of him, and she could see a piece of dark fabric tied above a tear in the jeans stained bright red. Limping! He had come around the rock limping.

"Is it cut?" she asked.

She glanced up at his face as he nodded, and her heart slammed against her ribs, making her suck in her breath.

God, but he was a handsome man.

"The windows blew out on the cabin," he said. "A big piece of glass hit my leg."

Emma frowned, forcing her eyes away from his face and back to his leg. "There might be glass in the cut yet," she said quietly.

"Maybe small pieces," he admitted. "I think I got the bigger ones out."

Emma shook her head. From the looks of the stain he'd lost a lot of blood. "I think we need to slit those jeans open to above the cut," she said, "and then tie the tourniquet directly on your leg."

He was silent a moment and then withdrew a pocketknife from his left pocket, his eyes meeting hers as he handed it to her. Green, green, beautiful green. His beautiful, pain-filled eyes.

Emma cleared her throat. "If I try to cut your jeans with this I'll end up opening your leg some more, too."

"So what do you propose we do?" he asked, and she heard the smile creep into his voice. He knew what to do just as well as she did, and he was teasing her.

Emma cleared her throat again. "I think you're going to have to take off your jeans."

"Damn, Ms. Kendrick!" he exclaimed appreciatively. "You're one smooth operator." He was grinning at her as he lay back, kicked off his shoes and untied the tourniquet. At the cessation of pressure, the wound started bleeding again, and Emma began pulling off his jeans as quickly as she could after he unzipped them. Together they retied the tourniquet, and she frowned at the cut. It was long and deep, and it was steadily pulsing blood. He would go into shock if it continued bleeding like this. And it must hurt like hell.

"Are you looking at my underwear?" he asked with interest as they worked over the cut. His fingers brushed hers as they both applied pressure to the cut with his handkerchief, and Emma felt her hand tremble.

"Of course not!" she said indignantly, only to find that her eyes immediately strayed upward and lighted on blue Jockey shorts.

Nice thighs. Very nice thighs. He was well-muscled from the work he did, and there wasn't an ounce of fat on him. Black hair feathered from thighs to knees where it became a denser thicket on long calves. Recklessly, Emma's eyes slid back up to the Jockey shorts and did the mental equivalent of clearing her throat. He was nice there, too. Emma lowered her eyes and tried to concentrate on the mission at hand, but she saw to her consternation that her fingers were still trembling. To cover her embarrassment she made a show of readjusting the tarp over their heads and nearly dumped a puddle of rain on them.

"My legs often throw women into confusion," he said, not unkindly, though he was still teasing her. He took over the tarp himself, and Emma dared a glance back at his leg, glad to see that the bleeding had definitely slowed. She fumbled with his pocketknife and flipped up a can opener, a screwdriver, and a corkscrew before he took the knife from her and opened the pen knife. He was about to take the jeans from her as well when Emma saw his hand falter and she glanced worriedly at his face. He was pale, and she quickly grabbed the knife back. She wished he'd groan and complain like a normal man and quit this silly stoic silence.

"I'll do it," she told him. "That way I can ogle your legs one more time."

"I'd have shaved them if I'd known you were going to be doing so much looking," he said, but the jest was half-hearted, and she saw him briefly close his eyes when he thought she wasn't looking.

"Here," she said when she'd opened the jeans from the tear all the way down. He reached for them but, worried again by the tight weariness around his eyes, Emma snatched them back and shook her head. "Lie back," she ordered him. "I'll put them on."

"Oh, God," he said, rolling his eyes.

"Do what I say," she said sternly.

"Yes, ma'am." He lay back with a sigh and held his legs up, one at a time, for her. "Tell me something," he said as she was easing them past the cut and tourniquet. "What do you do for a living? Run the state of Iowa?"

"And what does that mean?" Emma said, glaring at him as she let go of the jeans so he could make the final adjustments over his—very attractive—behind.

"It means you're efficient," he said, looking into her eyes. Emma found it very disconcerting to have him looking at her while she was still thinking about his attractive behind.

"Oh, sure," she said sarcastically. "I'm governor, and when I get back home I'm declaring war on Maryland." *If anybody ever finds us and I get home again.*

"So what do you do in Iowa besides be governor?" he asked. He was sitting up again, adjusting the jeans where they were cut.

"I run a store," she said shortly.

"Yeah? What kind of store?" He looked at her in interest.

Emma shrugged. "General merchandise. The kind of stuff people run out of at odd hours. Aspirin, ice cream, comic books, sunglasses. Kind of like the old five-and-dimes. My husband started it. He . . . died."

"I'm sorry," he said quietly. And after a short silence,

"Your husband—did you like this store he started?" He spoke hesitantly, like a man treading on uncertain ground.

Emma sighed. "Not at first. Doing anything yourself is hard work, and we put in more than our share of long hours. Sometimes we wouldn't see each other for days on end, it seemed. We took turns at the store. The Mercantile. That's its name."

"Nice," he said in a neutral tone. "But you got to liking it?" he prompted after she was silent awhile.

"In a way. I guess I like the people who come in. Kids who labor over counting out twenty cents for an ice-cream cone."

"Twenty cents? Dear God, Ms. Kendrick, you're giving them away."

She laughed. "I know. But there are too many things these days that are too expensive for kids. I didn't want to see ice-cream cones change like that. And then there are the old folks on a limited income who want to find a little something to give a granddaughter or a nephew on a birthday. I always try to have some good presents that aren't too high."

"So what kind of presents do you stock?" he asked. "I mean, if I came in the store looking for something to get you, what would you sell me?"

He didn't strike her as the kind of man who asked coy questions, so she thought a minute.

"Well, there's a whole rack of hair ribbons and barrettes and things, and I have this particular favorite. Now don't laugh," she warned him as his mouth twitched. "It's a dark-blue bow that fastens in the back of the hair, and it has two streamers that hang down about eight inches or so."

"So why haven't you gotten it for yourself?" he demanded, smiling at her.

"Because," she said impatiently, "it's for women with long hair, and my hair is very fine-textured so I have to wear it short."

He cocked his head at her critically, staring at her in the dark. "You have nice hair," he said. "It's soft."

"Thank you," she said dubiously. "But at the moment it looks like it belongs on a wet dog."

"Maybe we can dry you out some," he said and lifted the tarp edge to peer out. "The rain's almost stopped. I'll build us a fire."

Emma sat up straight in alarm. "Don't move! You'll make your leg bleed again."

He gave her one of those amused looks of his and said, "And I suppose you think you're going to build the fire."

"As a matter fact, yes," she retorted, wriggling out from under the tarp, all business as she began dragging over the wood he'd collected. "I was a Girl Scout once," she said over her shoulder. I hope he doesn't expect me to start this by rubbing two sticks together, she thought.

She nodded when he told her the fire would smoke with all that damp wood, and she began laying the wood several feet from the tarp. When she arranged the pile of wood to her satisfaction she glanced over her shoulder, and he reached into his pocket and tossed her a pack of waterproof matches. Well, that solved that problem. She got a smoky fire going and then hustled back to the tarp. She was shivering, and he drew her close to him against his left side, his hands massaging her upper arms. "There," he murmured into her hair. "Feel better?"

Yes and no. She was warmer, maybe a tad too warm. Being held close to him like this, feeling his big callused hands stroking her skin, was doing all kinds of things to her insides. She liked the feelings his touch evoked, but she was afraid that if he didn't stop she was going to say something stupid like *Don't stop.*

"There's one other thing," he said, serious now as his hands stilled.

"What?"

"I have to go back to the boat to get us some food and things. Now listen, and don't look at me like that. I brought a good long length of rope from the boat, so I'm going to tie it around my waist and swim out there. You hold onto this end of the rope."

Emma took a deep breath, her heart pounding so hard that she thought it would break a rib. He'd never make it with that gash in his leg. He'd lose too much blood before he ever got near the boat. She couldn't let him do it. "And what good am I on this end of the rope?" she demanded. "Do you really think I could pull you back if you got in trouble?"

He grinned and squeezed her arms. "Okay. We'll tie this end around the tree."

"Right. And when you start drifting out to sea you'll take that poor innocent tree with you. No."

He sighed. "Kendrick, this is no big deal. I brought the life vests. I'll just float out there and float back."

"No."

"What do you mean no?"

"No means no. I'm not going to watch you bleed to death in the middle of the Chesapeake." She got out from under the tarp and stood up. "I'm going." Even as she said it her knees were knocking together in tandem with her chattering teeth.

He snorted. "You can't go. You're afraid of the water. And besides, I won't let you."

"Oh, you won't," Emma said, eyeing him speculatively

as she found the life vest and put it on. Stubbornness was going to get her killed this time, she was sure of it. "Well, that's just fine," she said. "Maybe we ought to slug it out right here in front of the fire. Because, Rivers, that's what you're going to have to do to keep me from going. And I *don't* think you're the type who slugs women." What was she saying? He'd had no compunctions about hitting a football coach, had he?

He tightened his mouth and stared back at her, and Emma saw that he was assessing her determination and her fear. He probably thought she would back out once she got to the water anyway. Emma turned away and began fastening the rope around her waist.

"Come here," he commanded quietly. "At least let me tie a decent knot for you."

Her heart was quivering as his hands lingered at her waist, and it was only partly fear. She looked out at the water between her and the boat and wondered if she would die of fright or drowning.

"By the way," she said, her eyes narrowing. "How did I make it from the boat to here anyway? Did I have a sudden attack of bravery or something?"

He turned her around to check the rope, and she saw that he was smiling. "No, you didn't. I carried you."

"You carried me?" she repeated.

"I guess carried isn't just the right word," he admitted. "I sort of towed you while you floated on your back."

"Great. Now I feel like the *Queen Mary*."

He grinned up at her as he ran his hand between the rope and her waist, checking the slack. "Come down here a minute where I can see your eyes," he said, tugging on the rope.

Emma obediently knelt beside him, casting a surreptitious glance at his injured leg. No fresh blood. Good. "Now what, Rivers? Do you want to hear my last will and testament before I cast off?" She was trying to sound a lot braver than she felt.

"I know you're scared," he said, taking both her hands in his, turning serious. That was an understatement, she thought. She was terrified. But she didn't want him to know that, because he would insist on going himself, and bleed to death in the process. He was looking in her eyes, and Emma's fears faded. How gentle he was, she thought. For such a tall, muscled man with big, callused hands he had the manner of a lover who could give a woman one beautiful night to remember. Emma flushed and swallowed.

"I'll be all right," she assured him, unable to look away from his gaze.

"I know you will. The water's much calmer now and you have the life vest on and I'll be holding the rope. Just kick gently to push yourself to the boat. Don't struggle and tire yourself out. The vest will keep you afloat. Okay?"

"Rivers?" she asked, frowning.

"What?"

"Are there sharks in the Chesapeake?"

"No, the crabs ate them all." At the look of alarm on her face, he said, "Just kidding, okay? You'll be fine. Nothing will take a bite out of you. I guarantee it."

"I want you to promise me something if I don't make it," she said.

"You're going to make it," he told her, squeezing her hands.

"I know, but I want you to promise me anyway."

"Okay, okay, I promise. What is it?"

"Don't let Sunny eat that box of Godiva chocolates I have in my underwear drawer at home. Insist she bury them with me. And if Sunny says I won't miss just one—"

"God, you're a cutup, Kendrick," he said dryly.

She grinned at him, and a second later he gave her a crooked smile. "Godspeed, Kendrick," he murmured as she turned to leave.

Maybe it was her imagination, but as she waded into the water, her eyes grimly closed, she thought she heard him call softly, "I won't let anything happen to you," but it might have been a trick of the wind.

She walked on resolutely, stumbling over a rock, and then the water level reached her chest and she was floating, the rope buoying out behind her. For a moment she almost couldn't go on, but she took a deep breath and thought about him back on shore, the man who had gotten her to safety. It must have been an awful ordeal for him. The water would have been much choppier than this during the storm and his leg must have been hurting badly. And once on land, he had carried her several yards to the spot where she woke up. God, how had he managed it? He had promised to keep her safe just before the waterspout hit, and he had been faithful to that promise. She couldn't do any less now, she told herself. She fixed her eyes on the boat and began kicking her legs, slowly moving herself toward it.

This is just a little wading pool, she kept telling herself. *I'm almost to the other end of it.* To divert her mind further, she thought about Joel Rivers' green eyes and the feel of his hand on her skin. But that only succeeded in increasing the speed of her already racing heartbeat.

She frowned. She'd never had this physical response to Paul. Never a leap of the pulse at his look. But that all seemed so long ago now . . .

They had settled into a comfortable domesticity. Wasn't that what married people were supposed to do?

Sunny's words came back to her, words Sunny had said when Emma was in the hospital, her eyes swollen and red from crying. "Em, honey, it's okay to let yourself cry. I know you talked about divorce before, but you still lost your husband."

Had they ever been happy? She felt traitorous to Paul's memory to ask herself that. But it was something that hit her when she was lying in the hospital bed, a nagging question. Was that all there was to marriage and love? A simple, quiet life together—days filled with work, nights with a perfunctory kiss, and then deep sleep. Idle, unemotional talk about divorce. And then when your husband died you couldn't cry until months later. It wasn't Paul's fault that their marriage lacked excitement. It wasn't anybody's fault. It was just that they had made better friends than lovers.

And now that forbidden *something* was calling her. It was here now in the form of Joel Rivers, and Emma wanted to run away. She couldn't open her soul to that kind of blazing passion and then walk away from it. No, better not to tempt fate.

She had inched ever closer to the boat as her thoughts carried her along and now she came alongside it. She grasped the side and rested a minute before hauling herself over, hearing Rivers' triumphant shout on shore. She couldn't help it—she started grinning all over. Emma Kendrick, notorious chicken around water, had made it!

She kept the rope tied around her waist as she moved about on board, gingerly stepping over broken glass and splintered wood. She started in the cabin, gathering a cooking pot, some tins on the shelf, a few pieces of cutlery, and the plastic plates she found scattered on the floor. She loaded everything into a vinyl duffel bag lying under an overturned chair. She pulled the rope out the cabin door—

or what was left of the door—and looked around on deck. Her heart turned over when she saw the pool of blood and its trail to the cabin door. Near the steering rudder she saw his baseball cap lying in a puddle of water, and she put it into the duffel bag, too. Gingerly she plucked some crabs from the bushel basket that was still upright and dropped them in with her other booty. The other baskets had over-turned, and she could see crabs scurrying around in the corners of the deck, some of them making their way to the hole in the side and from there into the Chesapeake.

Emma took a deep breath, checked that her rope wasn't tangled on anything and then climbed back into the water. She held the duffel bag ahead of her as she doggedly paddled toward shore. He was sitting up, watching her every inch of the way, the end of the rope gripped tightly in his hand. He was leaning on his other hand and even at this distance Emma could see the drawn lines of pain on his face. *Damn.* She didn't want him to hurt. She wanted to take away his pain. But she was afraid to touch him. Afraid of what might happen . . .

Her eyes steadfastly fixed on him, she made the return trip quickly.

"So what did you do while I was gone?" she asked lightly as she dropped the duffel bag on the ground beside him.

"Tried to decide if you'd let me have one of those pieces of chocolate before I buried them with you," he retorted, and she saw the tension ease from his eyes.

"Not a chance," she said and looked down at his leg. There was some fresh blood. "How do you feel?" she asked, kneeling down.

"I'm fine." He was lying, and they both knew it. But since she couldn't do anything for him, she pretended to buy the lie. Nodding, she began unpacking the duffel bag.

"We'll do that later," he said in a husky voice. "You need to dry out. Here, get under here." He was holding open the tarp, and when she hesitated he made a tired attempt to wiggle his eyebrows at her. Emma smiled and crawled in beside him. He had both legs out straight, and he pulled her to his side so they were both facing the fire through the opening in the tarp. Emma began to feel warm again as he massaged her arms and pressed her against him. She let her head loll back on his shoulder—*just for a minute,* she told herself with massive self-control—and felt his heat stealing into her blood. Despite the smoke, the fire was warm, and she felt the most wonderful lethargy.

"Does your head still hurt?" he murmured, his fingers gently stroking her hair.

"A little," she admitted, giving herself over to his ministrations. It felt so good.

"Why don't you lie down?" he said, repositioning himself and drawing her down until she was curled on her side, her head resting in his lap.

"Your leg," she protested.

"You're not on it," he told her and continued his velvet assault on her senses. His fingers skimmed her neck and cheek and delved back into her hair, draining the tension from her body. Their exchange of words since they touched had been halting and short, as if both were troubled by the effect of their nearness. Now Emma realized how exhausted she was. She would just lie here a moment in the warmth of his embrace, she told herself. And then she would unload the duffel bag. Just a minute longer. He was so warm, his touch so soothing . . .

CHAPTER FIVE

When she awoke, Emma was curled on her side under the tarp, Joel's shirt rolled up under her head. She sat up quickly and pushed back the tarp. The dusk of the storm had given way to the dusk of approaching night. He was kneeling on one leg before the fire, his other leg, the injured one, held straight out to the side. His torso was bare, and her mouth went dry as she stared at the corded muscles of his back reflecting the dim glow of the fire.

"What are you doing?" she demanded in a sharp voice, worried about his leg.

He glanced over his shoulder, his gaze stopping on her face. "Fixing our dinner. How do you feel?"

"I'm fine," she said shortly. Her eyes fixed on his leg, and he shrugged.

"The food's almost done anyway," he said by way of explanation.

"I should have done that," she accused him. She could see the shadows of pain in his eyes. He was still watching her, and she realized she was clutching his shirt to her chest. "Here," she said in annoyance, standing up and carrying the shirt to him. "You'll freeze to death without this." A lump formed in her throat as his fingers brushed hers, and she tried not to watch as he pulled on the shirt. But she found herself drawn against her will to the sight of his lithe body. She frowned at the fire when he caught her looking at him. "So what's on the menu?" she said.

"Hungry, Kendrick?" he asked, grinning.

"I'll try to choke it down," she assured him.

He clucked in amused reproof as she hunkered down beside him. "I bet you've never had fresh crab before, have you?"

She shook her head doubtfully. "The only crab I've eaten came in a tin can and I mixed it with cream cheese and spread it on crackers."

"Lord, Kendrick, you're such an animal," he teased her. "Do you cook?"

"Of course I cook," she said indignantly. "I make a meatloaf that would make your taste buds roll over and weep with pleasure."

He laughed. "You'll have to fix it for me."

"As soon as we—" She broke off, having breached their unspoken agreement not to mention rescue.

He gave her a quick look before he began pulling the cutlery from the duffel bag. "They'll find us tomorrow," he said with deceptive assurance. He gave her another assessing look, then said, "I'm going to level with you, Kendrick. The marine radio isn't working. A chunk of wood took it out of commission." Emma vaguely remembered seeing the dented radio and a timber on the floor. "The CB works, but only on low power. We're too far from anything to raise someone on the CB right now, but tomorrow the boats will be back out and we can reach one of them." He gave her a nudge with his elbow. "You can hang on till tomorrow, can't you, Kendrick?"

"Not unless you feed me pretty quick," she said with more bravery than she felt. *What if no boats got in range of their CB?*

"All right," he said. "Sit right there, ma'am, and let the chef fill your plate." She sat cross-legged, inhaling the wonderful aromas as he lifted the lids on two pots balanced over rocks on the fire. When he handed her her plate it contained a boiled potato and a boiled crab, shell and all. Emma looked at him doubtfully.

"Relax, Kendrick. You're about to get a lesson on how to eat a crab."

It wasn't so difficult after all, she discovered, after he showed her how to open the apron on the back and extract the succulent meat. This was nothing like tinned crab! she thought as she licked her fingers. He was sucking the meat from one of the legs and laughing as he watched her imitate him.

Between them they ate all ten crabs she'd brought, and Emma leaned back in contentment, licking the juices from her lips. "Rivers," she told him earnestly, "you're going to make someone a great wife someday."

"Mere flattery from a starving woman," he told her, eyebrows arched as he opened another pot and produced a delectable mixed-fruit stew topped with biscuits.

"Dessert, too?" she asked, watching him with interest.

"Taste," he said, holding a spoonful to her mouth.

"Oooooh," she murmured. "Wonderful."

He lowered the spoon, but his eyes lingered on her mouth, and Emma was transfixed by the hunger of another sort on his face. Slowly he leaned toward her, and Emma held her breath, wanting him to touch her and at the same time knowing it would make her want him more than she had any right to want this man. His hand smoothed back her hair and his head came closer until she felt his breath fan her cheek. She was coiled like a steel spring inside. But as a sharp wind gusted and ruffled her hair, she abruptly turned her face away. Neither of them spoke for a long time, and Emma stared at the fire, listening to him rummaging through the duffel bag.

"Dinner was good," she said awkwardly when she trusted her voice again. She still wouldn't look at him.

"We hadn't eaten in a long time," he said casually, his back to her. Emma dared a glance in his direction and felt tears welling in her eyes. He was putting on the green cap he'd worn on the boat. This morning seemed an eternity away.

"So what do you think?" he asked, turning toward her and adjusting the cap. His smile was shadowy and didn't reach his eyes.

Emma pretended to consider the cap. It was much the worse for wear after the storm—wrinkled and still damp. "Well, you're not ready for any fashion show," she allowed, "but the casual look is in."

He began pulling the pots off the fire, his eyes shying away from hers. She knew he was thinking about the kiss that almost happened, and she could feel her heart pounding in her throat. If he'd known how much she wanted that kiss . . .

The wind had grown colder, and Emma wrapped her arms around herself. She looked at the sky, devoid of stars, and chewed her lip as she contemplated the bank of dark clouds building in the west. Another storm was coming. The prospect sent a chill through her and she shivered.

He noticed when he turned from the fire and he scooted closer to her, still holding his injured leg out straight. It was obvious from the grimace he tried to hide that the leg hurt him. Without speaking he took his Windbreaker and wrapped it around her shoulders, then took the edges of the jacket in his hands and looked her in the eyes.

"Another storm?" she asked, keeping her voice level.

He nodded. "We'll be all right under the tarp."

She stared back at him and finally voiced a fear that had

been lingering in the back of her mind since she'd returned from the boat. "What about the boat?" she asked.

He watched her face a moment, then said, "I don't know. It's got some bad damage. It may not survive the storm."

"And if it sinks, the CB goes down with it," she whispered.

"They'll find us, Kendrick. Don't worry."

But she did worry. It was something a minister's daughter did very well—worrying. And she had plenty to think about—what with the storm, the boat, and Rivers' leg.

The first splattering drops hit them, and Emma gritted her teeth. Dammit, she was going to get through this. She had to. He pulled the tarp over them again, enclosing them in the dark as the wind picked up force and raged around them. She began to lose track of time as they huddled there, buffeted by the wind, the pounding rain beating on the tarp. The sandy ground around them absorbed the water well, so little leaked in under the tarp. Still Emma was damp and cold and miserable. Adding to her misery was Rivers' nearness, his warmth radiating toward her. She had determined she would not let him hold her again, but when she heard his sharp intake of breath as he moved his leg she leaned toward him.

"Cold?" he murmured over the sound of the rain.

"Yes."

He put his arm around her, and she was careful not to lean on his leg. "Does your head hurt?" he asked.

"Not much." Neither of them mentioned his leg, because they both knew it was hurting and there no remedy for that. His hand moved up to her hair and gently stroked, and Emma felt a bond with him that she couldn't deny. She trusted him to keep her safe, as unrealistic as that belief was. He couldn't do anything about the storm or the boat if it sank, and yet she was sure that things would be okay as long as he was here with her.

"What was your husband like?" he asked abruptly, and she tried to see his face in the dark. He wasn't looking at her, but from the grim set of his jaw she knew he needed to talk to take his mind off the pain in his leg.

"He—Paul—worked hard," she began, trying to summon up all the images that were Paul, all the gestures and words that when put together would let this man see what her dead husband had been like. "Sometimes he would come home from work—he taught high-school science before we owned the store—and he would be so discouraged and tired that he looked ten years older. Paul was the kind of man who felt that if one kid in his class couldn't get the material then he'd failed as a teacher."

"Is that what made him buy a store?" Rivers asked.

Emma exhaled softly. "I used to think so."

"And now?" he prodded.

"Now I think—" she began. Then, "Hey, you sound like a psychologist, Rivers, you know that?"

She could feel him smile as his hand ruffled her hair. "Just the garden variety, Kendrick. Come on and tell me the rest. I'm listening."

"All right." She sighed. "Now I think Paul didn't know how to be happy with what he had no matter what it was." There. She'd said it. The worst thing she'd ever said about her husband.

"There are a lot of people in the world like that, Kendrick. I take it the store didn't help any."

"No." She remembered the long hours and Paul's feverish pace, work that seemed to get him nowhere closer to whatever it was he wanted. "No, it didn't. I think in the long run it just made him more unhappy. He'd still come home tired and discouraged, and he'd throw his jacket on the back of the kitchen chair . . . ." Her eyes filled with tears at the sudden, piercing memory that sprang to mind, the musty smell of the jacket after it hung in the store's closet all day, the chafing redness on Paul's jaw from the raw winter wind, the way his eyes always slid past her face and looked away from her. Somewhere along the way they had lost what brought them together.

The tears began slipping down her face and Emma roughly brushed at them with the back of her wrist.

"What did he look like?" Rivers asked softly.

"He was tall and stocky," she said, her voice quavering. "He was always dieting, always swearing off pizza or beer, and the next day he'd come home from work with a grocery bag filled with beer and pretzels and cookies. And he'd give me the most *sheepish* look, like I-know-I-shouldn't-do-this-but-don't-you-say-anything." She was laughing now, laughing through the tears, and Rivers' arm tightened around her. She heard him laugh, too, and then he said, "Go ahead and cry. You miss him."

And so she did, with her head on his shoulder and his fingers twined in her hair, stroking away her sorrow. She cried for Paul's death and for the things they had lost before he died. And with the rain pounding around them and the wind flailing the tarp she fell asleep, feeling secure with this man beside her.

She woke up abruptly as the wind screamed in fury. "It's all right, Emma," he said in his deep voice. "Go back to sleep."

"Joel, the storm . . ."

"Shhh. I think this is the worst of it."

She sat pressed close to him, savoring his warmth, and

she realized that this was the first time they had called each other by their first names.

He shifted his leg and Emma caught the grimace and barely suppressed groan. She had spent a few long, sleepless nights in the hospital, and her feelings of helplessness then were nothing compared to knowing that this man was hurting and she was powerless to do anything about it.

"While I'm on the subject of my life story," she said lightly, hoping to distract him, "have I told you what it's like growing up in a small town with a minister for a father?"

"Tell me," he said, ruffling her hair again, and she heard his relief that she would continue talking.

"A minister's child has to be beyond reproach," she said in a wicked imitation of Aunt Charlotte. "That's all Sunny and I heard from Dad's sister Charlotte. 'You two mind your Ps and Qs now.' She was big on manners. In Iowa a lapse in manners is a serious offense, right up there with stealing your neighbor's pig."

"Why do I have the feeling you two had a few little lapses?" he asked.

Emma grinned. "Enough to keep Aunt Charlotte fit to be tied about half the time. One time when Sunny was about four, one of our parishioners dropped by with an applesauce cake for us. As a widower, Dad was about the most eligible bachelor around those parts, and the single females in his congregation were always coming around on one errand or another. Well, Aunt Charlotte had a rating system for all the goodies they brought with them. She said that if Dad was going to remarry he might as well marry a good cook and spare her some work. Okay, so here Miss Lewis stood on our doorstep with her applesauce cake, and Sunny stretched up on tiptoe to look into the pan. And she shook her head and clucked like Aunt Charlotte and then she said, 'A mite stingy with the raisins, aren't we, Miss Lewis?' Just like Aunt Charlotte would say after Miss Lewis would leave."

Joel chuckled. "Tell me about you, Emma."

"Me." She pondered that one. "I guess that my worst occasions of sin were covering for Sunny. When she went someplace she wasn't supposed to go or snuck out of the house after we were supposed to be in bed, it was my job to do what I could to keep Aunt Charlotte from finding out. I'd make up outrageous stories if Aunt Charlotte discovered Sunny missing. 'She dropped her teddy bear out the window and went to get it,' I'd say, sweating with guilt during the whole lie. Or I'd swear that she had gone down to the kitchen to finish the peas she left on her plate at dinner."

Joel was laughing and Emma laughed, too, forgetting for the moment the howling wind and the ominous creak of the boat in the water.

"It sounds like you had a good childhood, Kendrick," he said, and she detected a note of wistfulness in his voice.

"I did," she agreed. "Sunny and I had Dad and Aunt Charlotte and a whole town filled with near aunts and uncles. Small towns are like that." She frowned, sensing his thoughts drifting away somewhere else. "Your turn, Rivers," she said, poking her finger at his shoulder.

"Not much to tell," he hedged.

"Oh, come on. And after I bared my soul to you."

She felt his reluctant smile. "Same story basically. Small town. Mom and Dad and a much older sister who now lives in Georgia."

He fell silent and Emma nudged his hip with her leg. "So what were your parents like?"

"Tired, tired, and tired," he said, ending on a sigh. "I guess you can understand that, after what you and . . . your husband went through with your store."

Emma nodded. "Was your dad a crabber too?" she ventured.

"Yeah. I grew up in the house where I live now. Crabbing was good in those days and the place was in pretty good shape. It's hard to keep up now, especially with me working all the time and . . ." He paused and cleared his throat. "Mike's medical bills ran pretty high and the insurance didn't cover them all."

"Was he in an accident?" Emma asked tentatively, figuring that given the situation they were in now they might as well ask personal questions.

For a minute she thought he wasn't going to answer, and his voice was filled with weariness when he finally did. "A car accident. He was only five. Hell, he'd just gotten a bike for Christmas." There was a fierceness in his tone, and Emma could sense the tears and frustration behind it. "Mike went to a Christmas play at school with his friend Robbie. Robbie's dad was driving, and he picked the boys up after he'd dropped into a tavern for a few beers. It's an old story—a little ice on the bridge, bald tires, Dave's reactions slowed, and the car ends up spinning around and slamming into the bridge's concrete wall. Mike got thrown into the front seat and damaged a lumbar vertebra." His voice was ragged. "The police came to the house and drove Brenda and me to the trauma center on the mainland. He'll live, the doctor told us the next day, but . . . It took me weeks after they said he'd never walk normally again before I could let go of the hope that he'd make a full recovery. I guess now I figure it's a miracle he can get around with braces. I admire that kid."

"Can I ask you something?" she ventured after a moment.

"Nope."

She was taken aback. "Oh."

"Come on, Kendrick," he said, bumping her with his shoulder. "I was just kidding. Ask me."

"I was just wondering if you and your wife—Brenda—if you got . . . I mean, if the accident . . . Oh damn. This isn't any of my business anyway."

He smiled and hugged her closer. "If we got divorced because of the accident?" he asked. "Is that what you want to know, Kendrick?"

"Well, yes." She supposed it was a roundabout way of asking if they'd been happy. A leftover remnant from her stay in the hospital when she couldn't stop turning her marriage over and over in her mind, wondering why she and Paul hadn't been happy before his death.

"You always hear about some tragedy bringing families closer together," he said pensively. " 'Tain't always so, Kendrick. Sometimes it rips a marriage right in two. In our case, I guess the accident was the heaviest stone in a load Brenda couldn't manage. And I wasn't any help for a month or so. Sat in the kitchen all night staring at the walls and not saying a word to her."

"But Mike lives with you," Emma said. "You must have gotten yourself together."

"Yeah. When he came home I was ready to accept what had happened. And we went from there. Brenda, unfortunately, went out the door."

"She walked out on the two of you?" Emma said, astonished.

"That's about the size of it. 'She needs a recovery period,' was how her parents put it, but later on she said it just wasn't going to work and the divorce papers came. I still blame myself for part of that."

"But why?"

"I'd seen what happened to my mother, and Brenda was a lot like her. Life isn't always beaches and sunshine here. People have to work hard to make a living. My mother had to work in the crab-packing plants, and it's hard and tedious and the hours are long. She just couldn't live like that. She was originally from the mainland and she'd grown up in a place where she was expected to learn how to cook nice meals and give nice parties and play bridge in the afternoon. She met my dad and her life was never the same. She worked so hard that my memory of her hands is of them cracked and bleeding."

"But she must have loved your father."

"Sometimes love isn't enough," he said wryly, and Emma felt his words penetrate her heart. He was right. Sometimes it took more.

"Brenda grew up on the island, but her parents wanted something more for her. It's only natural—all parents want their children to have more than they did." At that moment, Emma truly understood how hard it must be for him to want things for Mike that he couldn't have. "Well," he said wearily, "she thought she wanted the life of a waterman's wife. The accident only accelerated the end of the marriage. It was dying even before that."

Her marriage had been dying, too, Emma knew. Maybe it wasn't something she did or didn't do. Maybe it was just because it happened. And that was why she had cried so hard in the hospital, cried for something that had died long before Paul did.

"What about Mike?" Emma asked. "Does he spend part of his time with his mother?"

Joel was silent, and when she tried to see his face he turned away. "No," he said after a moment with more sadness than any man should have to feel. "She can't face how he is since the accident. She cries when she sees him, so she doesn't see him." He took off his green baseball cap and ran a hand through his hair. "Mike acts like it's okay. I don't know . . ." He tossed the cap on the ground and stifled a groan as he moved his leg. "Brenda and I weren't right for each other from the beginning," he said. "Everybody around here knew it, but I didn't listen." He turned back to her, a tired smile on his face. "I bet you never did anything you shouldn't, did you, Kendrick?"

Emma lifted her head but wouldn't look at him. "Oh, sure, I've done my share."

"No, I mean something big," he said impatiently.

"I certainly have," she retorted.

"Aw, come on. You, with your Iowa minister father?" He was dangerously close to grinning.

"You think I'm a paragon of virtue because my father is a minister, Rivers? Is that what you think?"

He shook his head, trying not to laugh. "No, Kendrick, it's because of—well, what you are."

"And just what am I?" she demanded, frowning in annoyance.

"You're . . ." He kept looking away from her and grinning, and Emma was ready to punch him in the shoulder for what he was probably thinking. "You're innocent, Kendrick, you know? I mean, you have this air about you. Like if somebody told an off-color joke around you, you'd blush and not say anything, but you'd spend the next seven days trying to figure out what it meant."

She did punch his shoulder then and he burst out laughing. "I am *not* innocent," she assured him.

"Mmm-hmm," he said, still grinning and thoroughly unconvinced. "So what's the worst thing you've ever done?"

Emma frowned down at her hands and then glowered at the tarp and the rain beyond. "I had an affair when I was nineteen," she informed him loftily.

"No sh—, I mean no kidding," he said, looking at her with interest. "So tell me about it."

"No!" she insisted, trying not to meet his eyes.

"Come on, Kendrick. You've got my curiosity up. Tell me the story. Was he good to you?"

"He was an irresponsible S.O.B.," she said in irritation, hoping to end the subject.

"God, he must have been something, Kendrick. You actually swore. So what happened? Did you both find someone else?"

"I'm sure *he* did," Emma said feelingly. "He left town."

His hand touched her chin and levered her face up until he was looking in her eyes. She could see the smile in his eyes but the sympathy, too. "Bad, huh?" he asked softly, his mouth crooking. "Did he hurt you, Emma?"

She sighed, content to look into his eyes for a long time. "I got over it," she said. "But it took awhile."

"You're amazing, you know that, Emma Kendrick?" he said, smiling into her face, his fingers lightly caressing her jaw.

"Not me," she assured him, looking away from his eyes before she did something foolish, like let him kiss her. Or kiss him first.

"Guess what?" he said, releasing her jaw and lifting up the edge of the tarp. "It stopped raining."

She leaned forward to see out, and although the water ran in rivulets across the ground the sky was clearing. A sprinkling of stars was visible in the west where the dark clouds had vanished. "The boat?" she asked anxiously.

He raised the tarp over his head, dumping a puddle of water onto them. Emma squealed and he shushed her. "Quiet! I'm trying to see if the boat's still afloat."

"I don't see what noise has to do with your vision," she muttered, but she lowered her voice. "Well?"

"Wait a minute," he told her, his hand motioning her impatiently. Emma chewed her lip and shivered, hoping that the boat hadn't gone to the bottom of the Bay, taking the CB with it. A dark cloud parted, and the moon rode into view, casting gray shadows over the shore. "There it is!" he said. "It didn't sink!"

In her relief Emma hugged him, mindful not to touch his leg, and the damp male smell of his skin assailed her nostrils. His hand found her hair and pressed her head to his neck. She wouldn't mind if he kissed her now, she really wouldn't. Because she was just so relieved that the boat was still there. And the kiss wouldn't be anything more than that. She waited, clinging to his neck, breathing in his scent, but finally she let go of him and he smiled at her, then turned away. Emma was disappointed.

The wood was too wet to start another fire, so they sat huddled together for warmth, the tarp around their shoulders. The last of the dark clouds scuttled before a light wind, and more stars rode high in the sky.

"You okay?" he asked her.

"Yeah. But my bottom's wet."

"Kendrick!" He was grinning.

"Because *you* dumped all the water from the tarp on top of us," she informed him.

He just grinned back at her.

Emma glanced out at the water. "Can the boat be fixed?"

"I don't know." He shook his head. "It needed engine work before we left and now this . . ."

"I guess your friend will have to fix it this time." She wanted to keep him talking—she'd seen how pale his face was and how often he tried to hide an expression of pain from her.

"Yeah, but knowing Dave he'll take his sweet time about it."

"Dave?" she said, startled. "But isn't he the man who was driving the car when . . . when the accident happened?"

"Yeah," he said.

"But he—I mean, how could—after all that—" she stammered.

He shrugged. "Dave put himself through hell over it, too. And Robbie was Mike's friend—any fool could see how miserable Mike was without Robbie around—so one day I called Dave and asked if Robbie could come over. Dave brought him and stood there at the door with tears in his eyes and whiskey on his breath. So I took him aside and told him that any man is entitled to one mistake, but he'd better not make another one with his son or I'd beat the crap out of him. He tried to clean up his act after that, but I don't know. The guy had it hard with his wife dying."

"You're amazing," she told him, repeating his words about her. "Joel Rivers, you are something else."

"Not me," he said, and grinned.

"I'm hungry," she murmured later, staring up at the stars. They had sat silently the last couple of hours, both exhausted, cold, and clammy. And he was still in pain.

"You want some of that fruit cobbler?"

"Oh, God, yes."

He smiled. "I like the way you get worked up about food, Kendrick."

He fixed them both some of the cobbler, but she noticed that he hardly touched his. He would close his eyes heavily at times and when he opened them again his jaw was tight and pale.

"Why don't you get some sleep?" he suggested after he'd put the cobbler back in the duffel bag.

"I'm not sleepy," she said.

"The hell you're not. You almost nodded off while you were eating."

"That was then. I'm not sleepy now," she insisted.

"Well, I am. Come here and put your head on my shoulder."

"And how's that supposed to help you sleep?" she demanded.

"I like the way it feels with your head on my shoulder. Now come here." So she scooted closer to him and leaned against his side, her head resting on his shoulder. "There now, isn't that better?" he asked in satisfaction.

"I'm still not sleepy," she said around a yawn, and he grinned, reaching over with his left hand to ruffle her hair.

When her eyes opened she saw the stars again. Despite her best efforts to stay awake for Joel she had slept after all. The sky was growing pale in the east. It must be close to dawn.

She lifted her head from Joel's shoulder to scan his face anxiously. She took in the haggard look around his eyes as he looked at her briefly, then turned his head away. He was pretending to look at the boat, but Emma knew he was trying not to let her see that his leg was worse. They had gently loosened the tourniquet several times, but still the wound bled and grew increasingly swollen and angry-looking. She knew it was critical now to get him to a hospital. They didn't have a lot of time left.

"See?" she said lightly. "I told you I wasn't sleepy."

When his head came back around he was smiling, but it was a tight smile, and his jaw, heavily shadowed with beard, was clenched. The dusky pre-dawn shadows made his eyes look distant.

"The watermen will be out soon," he said, and his raspy voice scared her.

"When can I go use the CB?" she asked, and he looked at her face intently for a moment. But her fear was secondary. Minutes were precious, and she simply had no time to be scared now.

"As soon as it's a little lighter," he said and closed his eyes on a suppressed groan.

"Am I supposed to have a handle or something?" she asked.

He opened his eyes. "A what?"

"You know. Don't CBers use weird nicknames?"

That coaxed a bit of a smile from him. "Call yourself anything you want. How about Fish?"

"Oh, now that's glamorous," she complained. "Why don't we just make it Crab?"

His smile turned into a grimace, and he looked away from her again and slowly eased himself down to the ground until he was lying on his back. *Damn. Hurry up, sunrise.*

He was silent a long time, his eyes closed, and Emma found herself clasping and unclasping her hands in her lap. "Emma?" he said quietly, his eyes still closed.

"What?"

"Don't worry."

"Oh, sure," she said stubbornly. "That's what I do

best." Then she added as an afterthought, "Other than swim to boats." He didn't smile, but his hand reached out and found hers, squeezing it tightly.

She kept staring at the lightening sky, holding his hand and wishing she could say something to help him. When she saw the first lavender rays of the sun, she said, "Joel?"

He opened his eyes with effort. "Yeah?"

"I think it's time."

"Okay. Here's what you do."

She felt no fear, only a desperate sense of urgency as she paddled in her life vest toward the boat. She kept glancing over her shoulder toward the shore, but, although he still held the rope in his hand, he was lying down, his eyes closed. *Hurry, hurry,* she told herself. She didn't realize how tired and weak she was until she had trouble hoisting herself over the side of the boat. Dragging the rope behind her, she went straight to the cabin and with shaking fingers flipped on the CB. Emma pressed the mike button. "Mayday, Mayday," she said. "We're beached on Crespin Island. We need help." *Please work.*

She released the button and listened through the static. *Please answer.* "We need help," she said into the mike again. "The storm wrecked our boat."

"Hey, little lady," a deep voice said when she released the button. "What's the problem there?"

Thank God. "We're beached—Crespin Island," she gasped out. "We need help. Hurry."

"Now calm down, honey. You run aground in your sail-boat or something?"

There was no sense of urgency in the man's voice, and the *honey* rankled. Emma's eroding patience was replaced with fury. "Now listen here and listen good," she said in a scathing voice. "I'm with Joel Rivers. His boat was wrecked in the storm and he's hurt. Now you'd damn well better get your can over here fast." She released the mike button with a snap and was met with a moment of silence. For heaven's sake, did he think this was a joke?

"Yes, ma'am," came the contrite voice. "Be there right fast."

She got back to Joel as quickly as she could paddle and found him breathing shallowly, his eyes closed. His face was ashen, and there was fresh blood around the tourniquet. "Emma?" he groaned.

"I'm right here." She took his hand and held it tightly.

"You reach anyone?"

"Yes, yes. They'll be right here."

"Did you tell them to hurry?"

"I think I made it pretty clear," she admitted, reaching out to stroke his hair.

She could hear the boat long before she could see it, and she stood up to scan the horizon anxiously. The two men had to put a dinghy in the water and row to shore, and Emma gently shook Joel's shoulder. "They're here," she said. "You're going to be okay."

"Hey," he said with effort, "you did all right, Kendrick."

"Tell me something I don't know," she told him, hiding her anxiety. He held onto her shoulders to ease himself to his feet and then leaned on her as he limped slowly toward the men debarking their dinghy.

"That you, Buckshot?" one of the men called, and Emma recognized the voice from the CB.

"Yeah, Shorty."

"What're you doin' here, man?" Shorty demanded.

"Just having a picnic," Joel said dryly just before he pitched forward and the two men caught him.

CHAPTER SIX

"Good evening, Mrs. Grundy," Emma called as she came down the staircase and started for the front door. "I'll be back later."

"Mmm-hmm," Mrs. Grundy said, wearing her usual expression, a frown that could mean anything from *You left waterspots on the glasses* to *I found a dustball in your room*. Right now Emma would bet the frown was more serious. Mrs. Grundy still suspected Emma of worse crimes than getting herself marooned on an island with Joel Rivers. In fact, the day the fishermen brought Emma back here, after taking Joel to the hospital and assuring themselves that he would be all right, Mrs. Grundy had looked down her nose at Emma and said, "Hear tell you went on a long picnic." Apparently, word of the boat accident and Joel's first words to Shorty had already traveled Thorn Haven twice over.

Emma hid her grin as she went out the door. Joel had come home from the hospital today, and it would be the first time she'd be alone with him since they were rescued from the island. She'd gone to see him in the hospital, but there were always three or four watermen sitting around on chairs turned backwards, and she hadn't done more than offer him a tentative wave of her hand and back out of the room. His eyes had sought hers over the heads of the other visitors, but he hadn't said anything.

During the days he was hospitalized, Emma called Sunny and told her she would take her up on that vacation idea and stay a little longer. Something made her refrain

89

from telling Sunny about the boat accident. Emma had checked on Cory and Mike every day, but Mrs. Gamble, a pleasant, grandmotherly type, had things well in hand.

To her surprise, Emma realized she was nervous about seeing Joel again as she drove over to his house. Stranded alone during a storm, huddled together for warmth, and she was nervous about seeing him? *You're a nut case, Emma Kendrick,* she told herself.

Still, the butterflies persisted as she knocked on the door. "Come on in—the door's open," came his voice from the open window upstairs.

"Well, here I am," she announced loudly downstairs, immediately wanting to thump herself on the head for sounding inanely cheerful.

"So get yourself up here," came his voice, filled with amusement.

Emma climbed the stairs and paused at the top to run a hand over her pink cableknit top and jeans. She had washed her hair that morning and let it air dry into soft layers around her face.

She cleared her throat as she peered into the first open door and saw him lying on top of the bedspread, a deck of cards set up for solitaire beside him. He looked so good that she didn't say anything at first. In faded jeans and a black cotton pullover, he was devastatingly handsome. His black hair was clean and combed and his jaw shaved.

"Hey," she said softly, giving an awkward wave.

"Hey, yourself, Kendrick." He grinned at her and motioned her to the bed. He was propped up against the headboard, and he moved higher to give her more room. She sat down on the edge of the bed and smiled tentatively. *Don't look at his eyes.* They were always her undoing.

"So—how are you doing?" she asked.

90

He nodded, lowering his head to try to see into her face. "Real good. How about you?"

"Not bad," she said. "In fact, I'm thinking about taking a shot at swimming the English Channel—what with all that water time under my belt. Of course I'm going to need a life vest and a duffel bag to do it—and a rope tied around my waist."

He laughed, and Emma found herself laughing with him. When they both fell silent, she stared down at the chenille bedspread, tracing a fuzzy line with her finger. Uncomfortable with the silence, she said, "Mrs. Grundy all but accused me of conjuring up that waterspout myself. Didn't approve of young women going off alone with men like that, she told me."

"Dear God—poor Mrs. Grundy," he said, smiling. "The only sin worse than that would be violating her kitchen rules."

"Well, I'm a scarlet woman in her eyes now," Emma assured him.

"Hey," he said, poking her hip with his sock-covered foot. "Didn't you promise me a dinner while we were shipwrecked?" He grinned broadly and twitched one brow upward.

"I don't think so," she said, trying not to smile. "I'm pretty sure I would have remembered that."

"Hey, now Kendrick," he said, his finger tapping her bare arm and playing havoc with her befuddled senses. He tried to adopt a stern expression. "I'm sure I remember something about you cooking me a dinner."

"Head injuries cause amnesia, you know," she said.

"And dessert," he hastened to add now that he had his advantage. "Apple pie for dessert."

"Whoa, Rivers!" she said, laughing. "Nothing was said about apple pie."

"Oh, Kendrick." He lowered his head and stole a look at her from under dark brows. "You wouldn't disappoint a man confined to bed, would you?" he asked hopefully. "Someone who'll have to eat peanut butter sandwiches because there's no one around to fix him decent food."

"You aren't allowed out of bed?" she said, concerned.

"Well, maybe the doctor said something about resting and not walking around too much." He was trying not to grin, and Emma swatted his foot.

"Okay," she said. "Dinner it is—and maybe dessert."

"I'm in rapture," he swore, placing his hand on his heart as she stood up, laughing. "You go ahead and I'll be down in a minute."

She started down the stairs and then thought to ask him if the boys would be back in time for dinner. She was almost to his room when she heard him talking on the telephone.

"Mrs. Gamble?" he murmured in an urgent undertone. "No, I can't speak up. Listen, this is Joel. I just wanted to let you know that you won't need to come by and fix dinner tonight. Okay, fine. See you tomorrow then."

Emma was back down the stairs before he hung up, grinning secretly to herself. So he'd have to eat peanut butter sandwiches, would he? The man was an incorrigible liar. But he obviously wanted her around—and that was nice.

She was breading the pork chops she'd found in the refrigerator when he came into the kitchen. He was limping slightly, and as he passed her on his way to a kitchen chair she caught a whiff of spicy cologne. She was glad then that she'd decided on the pink pullover instead of the more demure cream blouse she'd put on first.

He sat and watched her, and Emma grew warm under his gaze. She was thinking of how his arm had felt around her while they waited out the night during the storm. His touch had felt so right, but now she wondered if it had only been the storm and the fear that had made her think there might be something between them. He was certainly acting reserved now.

As if reading her thoughts he stood up and came up behind her. "How've you been, Emma?" he murmured, and her skin tingled in pleasure as she felt his breath on the nape of her neck.

"Okay," she told him quietly. *As long as you're with me.*

"I missed you," he said, his hand touching her hair. "I was about to climb out of the hospital window on a sheet. Why didn't you ever stay and talk to me?"

She shrugged, the slight movement brushing against his chest. Heat diffused her veins. "There were always so many people in your room," she said unsteadily. "I was . . . uncomfortable."

"Emma . . ." His fingers, gentle on her shoulders, turned her around to face him. She finally dragged her eyes up to his face and felt her throat struggling for air. Haunted green eyes, so lonely . . . so beautiful. His mouth moved as if to say something and then tightened. With a groan, he lowered his head to hers, and Emma's eyes closed heavily. A sigh was wrenched from her just as his lips brushed hers, softly at first and then hungrily. She had ached for this kiss all the nights he was in the hospital. She couldn't get enough of him, and she clutched his shirt at the waist.

His mouth grew demanding and her breath rasped. *Yes, more.* Her head fell back and he tangled his hands in her hair to hold her steady. His mouth was hungry and probing and Emma kissed him back fiercely. Unconsciously she pressed her lower body closer to him, her thighs feeling his hardness, a spur to her own arousal. Fingers still in her hair, his thumbs moved down to cup her jaw. He brushed his mouth tentatively over her face, exploring her jawline, the hollows of her cheeks, and her eyelids which trembled beneath his feathery kisses.

"Joel," she whispered raggedly. "Oh . . . yes."

"You feel so good, Emma," he murmured, his mouth making another distracted survey of hers. His tongue begged entrance, pushing and stroking the softness of her lower lip until her mouth yielded and drew him inside her warm recesses. His hands sought her waist, pushing up under her pullover, his rough hands gliding sensuously over her flesh, skimming her ribs until he touched her bra. He cupped her breasts and his thumbs boldly stroked her nipples through the lace, eliciting a moan from deep in her throat. "Touch me . . . yes," she urged him, straining her body toward his. She wanted to go back upstairs to his bed with him right now and she wondered in distraction if his leg was recovered enough. But Emma was an inventive woman, and she decided bad leg or not she could work around that. Oh, how she craved this man!

"Emma . . ." He was breathing hard and his hands left her breasts to tighten at her waist. She tried to re-capture his mouth, but he drew back, some unspoken anguish in his eyes.

"Joel?" she whispered. "What's wrong?"

The lines around his eyes deepened, and he looked weary—and miserable. "I want you so bad," he ground out, looking out the window over her shoulder instead of at her face.

"There's nothing wrong with that," she told him fiercely. "I want you, too."

"It's not right," he said.

Emma was bereft. She couldn't believe what she was

hearing. "Hey," she said shakily. "I'm the minister's daughter here and I'm not objecting."

He touched her chin lightly with his finger, a smile briefly playing at the corner of his mouth, and his eyes found hers. "You're the kind of woman a man . . . wants for keeps." Her heart froze at the desolate expression in his eyes. "I can't just take you to bed, Emma, and then say 'So long, it's been fun.' " She waited, knowing there was more. "I can't offer you anything, Emma. Don't you see?"

She shook her head, her hands withdrawing to hug herself. "No, I don't see," she said hoarsely.

"I can't let something get started that doesn't have a chance. Because, Emma . . . I can't ask you to share the kind of life I lead. It's not enough for a woman like you."

She understood then, and it was a cold knife in her heart. He was remembering his mother and Brenda, and he didn't want another woman to grow weary of the hard life he led and then leave him.

"I don't have any money," he said softly, his eyes beseeching her. "I couldn't . . . give you things. You'd have to work and work hard. I leave before sunup and I work at the tavern when I'm off. And . . . there's Mike. There are medical bills and the orthopedist and . . . You've seen how hard Mike struggles just to get out of a chair? That's our life."

"Money doesn't matter," she said. "Neither does hard work. And you and Mike have taught me more about courage than I've learned in the last twenty-nine years." She held up her hand. "And I never once proposed marriage to you."

He smiled sadly. "No," he agreed. "But you should be married, Emma. You should have a husband with the time and money to shower you with attention and a houseful of kids." He turned away and limped back to the chair.

The kitchen was silent except for the sizzle of the pork chops in the skillet. *Oh, Lord,* Emma thought. *Here it is again. The Henley Family Curse in triplicate.* One night stranded on an island with a man and I fall all over myself for him. And he tells me in a kindly voice that he can't marry me.

She was saved the ignominy of having him see her swipe at the tears of frustration that sprang to her eyes when someone knocked on the door.

Turning her back on Joel, she went to answer it. A tall man, with receding hair and a belly that hadn't quite gone to pot but was certainly padded, smiled at her in self-assurance. "So—you're Emma Kendrick, I take it?"

Emma frowned. "Yes."

"Louis Richter." He held out a meaty hand. "I coach at the camp. Mrs. Grundy said I'd catch you here. I have a permission form for Cory to make a trip to the mainland. Since he's . . . well, not staying with us anymore, that revokes the permission forms his mother signed."

"I see." She didn't step aside to let him in, wondering what it was about this man that made her dislike him on first sight.

"Hey, old man," Louis called over Emma's shoulder to Joel. "Heard you got a bad leg from an accident." He chuckled. "Maybe you can insist it was from playing football and impress some babes that way."

Babes? Now Emma knew why she didn't like him. From his derogatory name for women to the insolent way his eyes roved over her, he was an abomination to every female with two brain cells left in her head.

She stood aside stiffly as he walked past her, still chuckling. Joel didn't stand up, just nodded his head and said, "Hello, Louis," in a frosty tone. Emma gathered he didn't think much of Louis Richter either.

"Glad I caught you home, too, Rivers," Louis said, pulling another piece of paper from his pocket. "Got to get permission for our scorekeeper too. A one day trip's not too much for your boy, is it?"

"No," Joel said shortly, taking the paper Louis held out. Emma took the other one and signed it. Out of the corner of her eye she noticed that Louis kept shifting his weight from one foot to the other as if nervous, and there was a false heartiness in his voice.

"So," Louis said, stuffing both papers back in his pocket and shifting his eyes to Emma. "You going to be visiting Thorn Haven long?"

"I don't know," she hedged. She hadn't really thought very far ahead.

"With Rivers here laid out on his butt, maybe you need a tour guide," Louis suggested with a confident, oily smile.

"I don't think so, thank you," Emma said quickly.

"There's a good movie on tonight," he insisted. "One of those Rambo things. God, I love that guy."

Emma nodded weakly. "I'm sort of in the middle of cooking dinner now," she said.

"Go ahead if you want," Joel said in a expressionless tone, and Emma darted him a dark glance.

"Sure, why not?" Louis said, taking her irritated silence for assent. "I'll come pick you up at Mrs. Grundy's in an hour." He didn't wait for an answer, just opened the door and started out. "Watch out for that leg, Rivers," he called in parting.

Emma glared at Joel, but he was looking at the table and not her. "I don't need your help filling my social calendar," she informed him.

"You need to get out," he said.

"And Louis will conveniently keep me out of your hair?" she parried, aggravated that Joel was pawning her off on another man just because she had gotten under his skin.

"Aw, go have a good time," he said, standing up.

She would have said something else, but the boys came through the door just then. "Hey, wasn't that old Jerk Face leaving?" Cory said, nudging Mike and both giggling.

Joel gave them a stern look. "What have I told you about Louis?" he said.

"I know," Mike said, hiding his grin. "Don't call him names."

"Right," Joel said.

"Hey, what's for dinner?" Mike demanded, grinning openly at Emma.

"Pork chops," she told him, smiling back and liking this shy boy more and more. She began peeling potatoes to fry.

"Maybe we could go get some ice cream after dinner," Cory said hopefully.

"Your Aunt Emma is going to the movies with Louis after dinner," Joel said without looking at her.

"Oh, God, Em!" Cory cried with all the social censure he could muster with his ten-year-old voice. "Louis! *Gross!*"

Mike looked rather disappointed with her, too, and Emma felt a rising irritation with Joel. She wouldn't be going if he hadn't so neatly pushed her into it.

"I'd much rather go get ice cream with you," she told the boys, "but Mike's dad seems to feel I need more of a social life."

Mike threw his father a chastising look. "Geez, Dad. Louis?"

"You and Cory set the table now," Joel said, sidestepping the comment. "I need to call the marina to see if my engine's fixed." He limped out of the kitchen, and Emma stared after him, frowning, as the boys got out knives and forks and chattered together. Everything between Joel and her had been fine until that kiss in the kitchen. Then suddenly she was to be avoided like the plague. And she was not at all happy about being foisted off on Louis Richter, who, if Cory and Mike were to be believed, was a total jerk.

Twenty minutes later Emma was dishing up the dinner, and Joel still hadn't reappeared in the kitchen. The boys were praising each dish she set on the table, obviously thinking ahead to the apple dumplings she'd put in the oven a few minutes ago. Emma looked over the pork chops, fried potatoes, green beans, lettuce with bacon dressing, and biscuits and decided she'd done herself proud, culinarily speaking. "Dinner's on," she called to the house in general and then sat down at the table.

Joel came limping in, cast her a furtive glance and sat down. "Nice," he said quietly.

"I beg your pardon," Emma said, having heard precisely what he'd murmured.

He cleared his throat, still looking down at his plate. "I said this is nice."

"I'm so glad you like it," she said sweetly.

The boys looked from one to the other. "Hey, don't those dumplings smell good, Dad?" Mike said.

"Yeah," Joel said without enthusiasm. He was frowning over a biscuit as he buttered it.

"Maybe we could go out for ice cream after Mrs. Kendrick gets back," Mike suggested.

"Call me Emma," she told him. "And I'll probably get back too late. I'm sorry, Mike. Maybe we can do it tomorrow."

"Yeah," Mike and Cory said in unison, their enthusiasm intact, even if Joel's wasn't.

"Dad's never had someone like you around," Mike reported happily. "I mean a lady. Who can cook, too. He used to go out on dates sometimes, but not anymore."

"Mike, I don't think Emma needs a complete rundown on my social life," Joel told his son, and Emma could swear a red flush was seeping into the hollows of his cheeks.

"Aw, come on, Dad," Mike protested. "I mean, Emma might decide to leave if we don't treat her nice. And then we'll be stuck with just Mrs. Gamble again."

"Mrs. Gamble is a nice, capable woman," Joel said.

Cory rolled his eyes. "Yeah, but she doesn't *understand* us. She makes us eat bran muffins every morning and she says to wash our hair every night and she doesn't ever want to go out for ice cream."

Emma couldn't help smiling.

Joel was shaking his head over his plate. "The boys hardly say two words most of the time," he muttered, almost to himself. "Now suddenly they're trying out for *The Phil Donahue Show*."

Emma glanced at her watch and stood up, and Joel rose with her. "Sit down. I've got to be going." She started for the back door, and Joel followed her outside onto the porch. Charles the cat was engaged in personal grooming near the door, one paw vigorously rubbing an ear. "Well, hello, Charles," Emma said, bending to stroke the cat's back. He arched against her hand and purred loudly.

"I still think you bought him off," Joel said irritably. "That cat acts like I'm Genghis Khan."

"No," Emma concluded. "He's probably just PO'd with you which is what I am at the moment."

"Emma . . ." He had that same look on his face he'd had when she set off into the Chesapeake, the rope around her waist. Only there was no rope around her waist now. He never finished whatever it was he was going to say, and Emma went down the steps toward her car. She looked back once, in time to see Charles stalk huffily past Joel, pausing only long enough to cuff his ankle with one paw.

Well, Emma thought despondently, she had to keep this date with Louis, but she sure as heck wasn't going to enjoy it.

As it turned out, Emma needn't have worried about inadvertently enjoying herself—Louis was as much a jerk on a date as he had been in Joel's kitchen.

He talked all through the movie, which wouldn't have been so bad if his comments hadn't voiced particular enthusiasm for the more violent scenes. He asked Emma if she wanted anything from the snack bar and when she said a chocolate bar might be nice he told her sugar wasn't healthy, shaking his head sagely. Emma told him she'd risk it.

He came back with a soda for each of them, and Emma looked at the cup and then him. "Carrot juice?" she ventured dryly.

He gave her a puzzled frown and then laughed. "Hey, that's pretty good," he said, looping his arm around her as he sat back in his seat. Emma extricated herself from his arm by bending over and pretending to need a tissue from her purse and then repositioning herself.

Louis took her out to a small restaurant after the movie, raving about the salad bar. He tried to put his arm around her shoulder again as they entered the restaurant, and Emma stiffened under his touch. "Hey, Arnie!" he called to a man across the room, propelling Emma toward Arnie's table.

Arnie, a burly, clean-shaven man who looked like he

could have wrestled professionally, stood up and high-fived Louis. "Arnie used to play proball for the Cowboys," Louis told Emma, in a tone of voice that said she should clearly be impressed.

"Got cut right out of training camp," Arnie told her mournfully.

"Well, I hope the cut healed all right," Emma said, pretending to be dumber than she was.

Both men stared at her and then Louis laughed. "Great little kidder. So, Arnie, since you're eating alone, can we join you?"

"Are you sure you don't want to be alone?" Arnie said, giving Emma a suggestive raise of his brows.

"The more the merrier," Emma said fervently.

Arnie and Louis settled down to serious talk after they'd gone back for second helpings at the salad bar, and Emma stifled a yawn as they discussed professional football. Then she heard Joel's name.

Louis was laughing. "It's pathetic, that kid of his, sitting there on the sidelines with the score book. Like it doesn't matter that he'll never be a football player."

Arnie shrugged. "Rivers ought to find himself another wife and have a kid who'll be able to do something. A man can't feel like much with a kid like that."

Emma felt pure, cold fury filling every pore. "Take me home," she said to Louis coldly.

"Huh?" he said, looking at her in surprise.

"Now," she said, standing up. "Take me home."

"Hey, what's going on?" Louis demanded.

"What's going on is that two grown men are talking about a boy as if he had no worth. For your information, Mike Rivers is more of a man with his handicap than either of you will ever be no matter how many Rambo movies you see." It was a long speech for Emma, and she finished on a breathless note. "Home. Now. You do understand that, don't you, Louis?"

"Yeah, sure," he mumbled, standing and giving Arnie a helpless shrug that said *Women, go figure.*

"Mrs. Kendrick, Mr. Rivers is here to see you, I believe," Mrs. Grundy announced from the kitchen doorway. It was the morning after Emma's date/ordeal with Louis, and Emma was feeling none too kindly toward Joel for his part in it. She was just about to sit down to a breakfast of scrambled eggs, toast, and coffee, and she frowned.

"What does he want?" Emma asked.

"He didn't say," Mrs. Grundy sniffed, eyeing Emma's short yellow batiste nightshirt with the white ruffles and the matching robe that was just as diaphanous.

"Well, it had better be important," Emma warned no one in particular, tying her sash in businesslike gestures as she strode into the hall in her Mickey Mouse slippers.

He was standing just outside the front door, his back to her as he stared off toward his own house. "What?" she demanded, halting on the threshold.

He turned around, taking a quick look at the healthy length of bare thigh showing between the folds of her robe and then looking off to the side, frowning. "The boys were wondering . . . that is, *I* was wondering if you were busy today."

"Why?" she snapped. "Is this another one of your cute little initiation pranks?"

"Pranks?" he repeated, looking back at her curiously.

Emma nodded vigorously. "That was the whole idea of sending me out with Louis last night, wasn't it? It had to be a joke, right? I mean no one in her right mind would voluntarily spend time with that . . . that . . ."

"Hey, you had a bad time," he said. Then he looked pleased. "Didn't you?"

"Of course I did," she snapped. "What did you expect?"

He shrugged. "I don't know."

"Well, I'd appreciate it if you wouldn't do that anymore." She glared up at him and found him sneaking another look at her legs.

"Do what?" he said in distraction, looking away again.

"Fix me up on dates just because you're too chicken to be around me," she retorted.

"Oh, that."

"Yeah, that."

He cleared his throat. "Well, listen. About today. How about going out for some ice cream?"

"Is this you asking?" she said. "Or are you setting me up with the boys?"

He grinned and tried to stop but wasn't too successful. "The boys are coming, too—but I'm asking."

"Well, all right then."

"All right then," he repeated. He grinned at her some more, and then he looked at her legs openly. "You sure know how to get a man's blood pumping, Kendrick," he said admiringly. "I'll pick you up in about an hour."

He left her to digest his compliment while he walked back toward his house whistling. Emma smiled as she watched him saunter away. *Well, all right.*

CHAPTER SEVEN

He was there in his pickup truck, right on time, and Emma let the curtain drop so he wouldn't know she'd been waiting. She frowned into Mrs. Grundy's hall mirror and stood on tiptoe to see as much of her outfit as she could. There being no defined rules for apparel when getting an ice-cream cone, she had dressed casually in blue shorts, a white T-shirt, and sandals.

"In the back, boys," Joel called cheerfully to Mike and Cory as he hopped out of the truck. He waved at Emma who had come outside and then proceeded to trot to the back of the truck and lower the tailgate. Her heart leaped to her throat as she saw Mike round the truck on his crutches, but Joel casually picked him up and set him down inside the camper shell. "You next, wild one," he told Cory, swinging him up to join Mike. "Repeat the rules," he ordered.

"Sit still and don't make too much noise!" the boys parroted back, giggling, and Emma knew this was a ritual of theirs. He slammed the tailgate shut and turned to Emma, grinning.

"I don't know the rules," she said innocently.

He took off his green baseball cap and ran his arm across his brow, taming the grin. "Well," he said, looking back at her. "How about sit close to the driver and smile a lot?"

"Sounds tough," she told him, trying not to smile.

"Do your best, kid," he advised her, limping to her and taking her arm. He escorted her to the passenger side and handed her in, giving her another grin as he shut the door.

He was up to something—she just didn't know what.

They pulled away, and he patted the expanse of seat between them. "Come over here," he said.

"I think I'll stay put," she told him with arched brows.

He manufactured a disappointed sigh for her benefit and said, "I'm still on your list, right?" When she didn't answer, he said, "Look in the glove compartment."

"What for?"

"Damn, Kendrick, you're a suspicious woman. Now look in the glove compartment."

She still wasn't sure she ought to do it. She never knew what he was up to. Bracing herself, she twisted the knob and the little door fell open. "And what did you want from here?" she said. "The maps, the flashlight or the petrified chewing gum?"

"The white box," he told her patiently, glancing over long enough to roll his eyes at her.

She took out the box and held it, frowning.

"Well, come on! Open it!"

Emma sighed and cautiously lifted the lid. The wonderful aroma of chocolate assailed her, and she stared down at the creamy fudge. "Oooooh," she said despite her attempts to remain reserved.

"I did good, huh, Kendrick?" He couldn't stop grinning, it seemed.

She had to agree. "Yeah, Rivers. You did great."

He was basking in her grudging praise, and she turned and looked out the window to hide her smile. He was always surprising her. She broke off a piece of the fudge and savored it. "Oh, yes," she murmured, closing her eyes. "This is good."

He cleared his throat. "You wouldn't want to pass a piece over this way, would you?"

She gave him such a woeful expression that he laughed, but Emma broke off another piece and handed it to him. "Now," she said. "Is the fudge your way of making up for Louis?"

He considered a moment. "Actually, I'm hoping to buy your good will." He popped the fudge in his mouth and glanced at her sideways.

Emma's brows rose. "And why would that be necessary?"

He didn't say anything for a minute, then he asked, "Are you still planning on taking Cory home before camp's over?"

He wouldn't look at her and Emma felt the seconds ticking away as she tried to decide what to answer. She didn't know. She'd have to play this one by ear. Her instincts told her that a lot was hinging on her answer, that this mattered to Joel Rivers a great deal.

"I haven't had much time to think about it," she said finally. "It doesn't seem to be as . . . urgent now." She frowned, thinking of Louis's cruel remark about Mike last night.

"I wish you'd let Cory stay until camp's over," he said, still not looking at her. "He's done a world of good for Mike. He accepts Mike just the way he is, something my son hasn't experienced here on Thorn Haven where everyone knew him before the accident. And I think Mike's been good for Cory. They're both opening up more."

Emma could see that he was right. The two boys had become fast friends, and they were good for each other. "When's camp over?" she asked. He glanced at her, and now it was her turn to look the other way.

"Another six weeks."

She took a deep breath and nodded. "All right."

"Emma . . ." He stopped, and she waited for him to continue. "Will you stay, too?"

When she hazarded a look at his face, he was staring back out the window, his features set as if to receive some invisible blow. If his eyes hadn't been so sad or tired or if it hadn't been so obvious how much he loved his son she might have been able to go home to Iowa and assure her escape from the Henley Family Curse. But he was all of those things, and she couldn't make herself leave right now.

"I'll stay . . . for a while anyway."

"Really?" He looked over at her quickly, the tension draining from his face.

"Despite the fact that you wanted to get rid of me last night," she couldn't help adding.

"Emma, it's not that I don't want you around," he told her softly. "Lord knows it's the opposite. And that's why I can't risk what almost happened with us last night." He frowned. "But I don't want you running back to Iowa either. You're . . . special. And I don't want to let you go." He gave her a lingering assessment. "I can't lie to you. You know as well as I do that I can't offer you anything more than . . . friendship. It's not fair to you."

Oh, Lord. How was she supposed to live with friendship when all she could think about was his arms around her, feeling so right? "So what are we going to do?" she murmured weakly.

"New rules!" he announced, trying to make her smile.

He succeeded and he leaned back, beginning what she knew he'd thought about a lot since last night. "No more kissing, all right?"

It wasn't all right, but she nodded anyway, figuring she'd hear his list of rules and then tell him why they wouldn't work.

"And no more us being alone, because I don't trust you." He gave her a gentle punch on the shoulder when she would have disagreed. He was grinning again, and she was ready to throttle him and all his rules.

"And?" she prodded, knowing there had to be more.

"And you can't get mad at me," he finished.

"Can't get mad at you?" she repeated incredulously. She stared out the window and tried to count to ten because she was mad at him already. The land was flat and marshy and gulls cried as they dipped down to stand gingerly on fence rails. There was something almost mournful about this land.

"Just this once," he assured her. "You can get mad another time if you want."

"And why would I be mad now?" she demanded, not sure she wanted to know.

"Because this is more than an ice cream outing. We're going on a picnic."

She couldn't get mad at him though she tried. It was a perfect day for a picnic, and it gave her an excuse to be near him. She leaned her elbow on the truck door and rested her head against her hand. "So the fudge was just to set me up for all this," she said.

"Well, did it work?"

She thought about it a minute, then said, "All right, Rivers. We'll try your little set of rules and I won't get mad at you for the picnic and Cory and I will stay here a while longer. Okay?"

"Hey!" He rapped his knuckles on the window behind them and hollered, "She said okay! Cory can stay!" The boys whooped and bounced up and down, making Joel call out, "Remember the rules!"

All right, Emma thought. *We'll see how good he is at remembering his own rules.*

* * * * *

He took them to a section of sandy beach on the other side of the island, a place he said the tourists hadn't found yet because it was too far from the restaurants and gas stations. He got out of the truck and limped around to help her out, his grin widening. "Here," he said, tugging her away from the truck and making her stand facing the blue expanse of the Chesapeake. He got behind her and put his hands on her shoulders. "Now I want to hear some proper admiration," he told her.

"Ooooooh," she said, teasing him.

"Not as good as the fudge, but it'll do," he decided, ruffling her hair and heading back to the truck. He lifted the boys down from the camper and began unloading a picnic basket and a blanket. Mike stumbled a bit on the sand, and Emma had to force herself to stand still and not run to help him, but she managed and he was soon finding his balance and swinging his legs through the crutches. The blanket and picnic basket were deposited on a strip of warm sand and then Joel was pulling her toward the water. He kicked off his tennis shoes and she saw he was sockless. So she tossed her own sandals over her shoulders and went running toward the water, feeling more free than she had in ages. Was this what people meant when they talked of being renewed?

The two of them stopped after they'd waded ankle-deep into the cool water, soft mud oozing beneath their feet. Emma closed her eyes and drew a deep breath of tangy, fresh air, then looked around appreciatively. The island arced back into the Bay at the far end, and a cluster of dark, lonely pines stood vigil. On the other side the land was flat and barren, melting into marsh farther inland. The Chesapeake itself was a blue-green, like morning grass seen through the dew.

"Are you okay?" he asked quietly at her side, and she nodded. The boys were walking by the water farther down the shore, and she smiled at them. She could understand why Cory wanted to stay here a while longer. She'd like that herself . . .

She took another gulp of air, feeling it float through her like an intoxicating drink, and stood silently, letting the breeze play with her hair.

"What are you thinking?" he asked.

What had come into her mind was the picture of that osprey she had seen the first day at the ferry and the strange exhilaration she'd felt watching him soar and dive. Inside, her soul was following the osprey's flight.

But she decided to tease him instead. "I was wondering if I still get to keep my fudge since I've agreed to your rules," she said, and a slow grin spread over his face.

"That'll cost you, Kendrick," he warned her, a glint stealing into his eyes.

She laughed and took off running down the sand parallel to the water, and he hollered behind her, giving chase. She could hear the smack of bare feet on wet sand and knew he was gaining on her, and her heart pounded with excitement. His fingers touched her shoulder, and as he drew parallel with her their feet tangled and they went down, laughing.

He had pulled her to him when they began falling, and now she landed on top of him, finding herself looking into a pair of lazy, teasing green eyes. "You okay?" he asked, brushing a lock of hair from her cheek.

Emma nodded. "Your leg?" she asked immediately, shifting her weight away from it.

"It's fine," he assured her. "Believe me, Kendrick, you're a slow runner." More like he was in incredible shape if he caught up to her with his injured leg, but at the moment it wasn't important. What mattered right now was the feel of his hard, masculine body beneath her softer one. What mattered was that her breath was feathering in and out like her heartbeat, and she could see the light of burgeoning desire in his eyes. Oh, yes. Those beautiful eyes gave him away. He wanted her, and that knowledge made Emma almost reckless with longing.

The water rippled with a sound like a sigh just a few feet from them, and a gull gave a half-mournful, half-outraged cry that hung in the air. The breeze laid little drops of dewy moisture on her face. But she concentrated on the face so close to her own. Her hands had come to rest on his shoulders and she couldn't seem to stop her fingers from beginning a zephyr-like caress of the muscles beneath. Their laughter had carried off on the wind, and now even breathing was suspended. His hands held her waist, so still and strong. Ever so slowly he lowered her until her breasts rested on his chest and her hair brushed his cheek. She could feel their heartbeats fusing like two powerful currents forced into sudden proximity.

She turned her head slightly . . . just enough to make her lips brush his jaw. "You're bad, Kendrick," he told her with a soft groan, and she laughed. "You're trying to make me break the rules."

"They're *your* rules," she reminded him, one finger trailing down the side of his neck.

"Yeah," he said with profound regret in his voice. "So they are." His hands slid to her back and stroked her hips. "And you're one devious lady, Kendrick."

"Me?" she said innocently, all eyes and sweet smile as she raised her head to look at him. "A minister's daughter?"

He gave a low grunt, and she could see wry amusement in those eyes. "Come on, Kendrick, and 'fess up. Your dad's really a corporate raider or something, right? Because you're too full of the devil to be a preacher's kid . . ." He rolled her to her side on the sand and leaned over her, looking dark and dangerous with the sun sparkling behind him. "And you're far too fond of chocolate and men who aren't any good for you." The last was said seriously, and she inhaled sharply and held it. His face was so close, and for a minute she thought he might kiss her after all. But he touched her nose lightly with his finger and grinned. "And I'm going to dump you in the Chesapeake and wash some of that mischief out of your lovely head." He scooped her up before she realized what was happening and held her close to his chest as he walked toward the water, slightly favoring his right leg. He was grinning a grin to beat the band, and Emma couldn't help laughing. He was just as incorrigible as she was.

She closed her eyes and squealed as he made as if to drop her in the water, but instead he swung her legs down until she was standing ankle-deep in the teal shallows of the Bay, her hands still laced behind his neck. And there were his eyes again, watching her and laughing in their green depths.

"Hey, Dad!" Mike called, and they both turned to see him balancing on his crutches farther up the beach. "Come see the crabs."

"Crabs?" Emma said in some small alarm, immediately dancing on her toes.

Joel laughed and took her hand, pulling her from the water. "Ghost crabs," he informed her. "They're more afraid of you than you are of them."

"Well, I just hope they're aware of that fact," Emma said, walking back toward the boys with him.

Mike proudly pointed out one of the crabs to Emma as it

scuttled to a hole in the sand with the speed and near-invisibility of smoke on the wind. And Cory dug up a tiny horseshoe crab no bigger than a button to show her. A minute later the boys were off exploring something else, and Emma and Joel settled down on the blanket. She watched the boys, and she couldn't help thinking about Louis's remark.

"Joel?" she said tentatively looking over from her cross-legged position to where he reclined, his hands behind his head.

"Hmmmm?"

"Do you really think this football camp is the best thing for the boys?"

He didn't say anything, but she frowned out at the Bay when he turned his head to look at her. "Why?" he asked softly.

Emma shrugged and stared down at her hands. "It just doesn't seem the healthiest . . . well, atmosphere for young boys. What with Louis Richter," she added lamely. She darted a quick glance in his direction and saw him studying her carefully. She supposed he must know what she was getting at. Other people, thoughtless people, must have said things about Mike. It was sad, but unavoidable.

"I can't shelter Mike from everything," he said softly. "Even from someone like Richter. Mike has to make his own choices and deal with all the crap the world can dump on a kid like him."

She looked over at him again, feeling a terrible sense of the pain father and son went through together. And both were so strong and so . . . proud. Joel Rivers was someone who could impart courage with his touch and his look.

"Hell," he swore softly, sitting up and stretching his back. "Richter isn't the worst thing Mike's ever going to have to face. But he sure as hell makes a lot of other things look good." He didn't say anything for a minute, just looked out at the water and then, so quietly she almost didn't hear him, "Did Richter say something to you last night, Emma?"

"Nothing, really," she lied, avoiding his eyes. "He was just being a jerk."

"Yeah," Joel said, leaning back. "Now there's something he's good at."

Mrs. Gamble was brewing hot tea when they got back that evening and Emma came inside with Joel and the boys. "Got some sun, did you?" Mrs. Gamble asked in her squeaky voice, patting Emma's sun-flushed cheek. "You look wonderful, child. Now, before you do anything, go call that sister of yours. She phoned earlier and she wants to talk to you."

Emma looked at Joel and he said, "Use the phone in the living room if you want."

She excused herself and dialed Sunny, trying to decide what Sunny could want now. Emma had already assured her that everything was fine here.

"Em!" Sunny squealed when she'd dispensed with the formalities of asking how her sister was. "The man from the bank called today—on Sunday, yes. That's how important it is. He has an even better buyer for the store. More money, Em! Now what do you say to that?"

Oh, Lord. What was she supposed to say? That she was thrilled? Well, she wasn't. The store was the one thing she could call her own, the one solid thing left in her life, and now she was supposed to turn it over to strangers. No, she wasn't thrilled.

"Listen, Sunny," she said wearily. "Can you stall the

bank? Tell them I'm out of town and won't be back for a while?"

"Why, Em? I thought you'd be excited."

"I don't know. I just feel so . . . unsettled. I need time."

"Well, okay, if that's what you're sure you want."

"Yes, please, Sunny. Thanks."

She stood there staring at the phone after she hung up, thinking.

"Emma?" She turned around, startled, and saw Joel standing right behind her. "Is everything all right?" he asked, nodding toward the phone.

"Yes, I suppose so," she said wearily. She looked in his face, trying to read his expression. "Sunny said the bank called with a good offer on the store."

When she didn't elaborate, he said, "I didn't know you were trying to sell it."

"That's just it," she said, raising her hands in an ambivalent gesture. "I wasn't, but Paul took out such a large mortgage on it that I'm having trouble making payments. And his life insurance largely went to pay off our house. The bank has been after me for a while now to sell the store."

"I'm sorry," he said with genuine regret. "That must be hard."

Emma nodded. He was no stranger to financial straits himself. "If I sell I can pay off what I owe on the store, but I won't have anything left, certainly not enough money to make a new start on something else." Slowly she sank down on the chair by the phone. "Isn't that funny?" she said wryly. "Here I am not quite thirty yet, and I don't know what I want. And I'm facing the dangerous possibility of losing what little I do have."

She wasn't going to cry in front of him, but her eyes filled with tears anyway and she ran her hand across her face to hide them. "Hey," he said softly, kneeling down in front of her. "It's not so bad, Emma. Money isn't everything."

"No," she agreed, shaking her head, covering his hand with hers when he placed it gently on her knee. "It's easier to say that when you have some, though."

He laughed quietly. "Yeah, you're right there."

"Money wasn't even what I wanted at all when I married Paul," she said in a low voice, wondering even as she spoke why she was telling him this. After their boat accident she seemed to tell him things she'd never said aloud to anyone else. "I just wanted someone . . . someone for me. And a baby or two to watch grow up and laugh with and play with." She sighed shakily. "It didn't seem like a lot," she marveled now, looking back on the past. Her eyes focused on Joel's face, and she saw his beautiful eyes, so lonely, intent on her face, his mouth softened in sadness for her. His hand moved beneath hers, twining their fingers together. "Once Paul bought the store there just wasn't any time for us anymore," she mourned. She was silent a minute. "I didn't even get my babies." She tried not to sound so sad and bereft, but those emotions seemed determined to come out. "I'm a pretty good bookkeeper," she said, "and I can run the fuel assistance program better than anybody, and that's my life." And now this, she thought, looking away from his face. *I think I'm falling in love with you.* One more thing she couldn't have.

"You'll find somebody, Emma," he told her gently, and there was pain in his voice. "Somebody who will give you babies and a good life." He wouldn't look her in the eyes now, and she mourned what both of them missed.

"Confession is supposed to be good for the soul," she murmured, mustering a smile for him. "All it does for me is make me hungry."

He smiled then, too. "You're always hungry, Kendrick. Come on. You can share your fudge with me."

"Fat chance," she assured him as he pulled her to her feet, and they both laughed.

Emma dawdled at Joel's that evening, loving the feel of his house with Mrs. Gamble bustling around, insisting on doling out more cookies for everyone and hopping to her feet the second anyone swallowed the last iced tea in their glass. Twilight waned, and with the dusk the whir of cicadas in the trees gave way to crickets and katydids.

It was time for Mike to do some of his physical therapy exercises, a nightly ritual, and Joel went upstairs with him. It was another thing Emma loved about Joel. Tomorrow was Monday, and he had to be on the water before dawn, but there was no question that his son came first. Mike was still shy about anyone but his father seeing him do the exercises. They were designed to stretch Mike's muscles and build strength in his upper torso, and Joel had told her it was difficult for him to watch Mike work and strain so hard that perspiration soaked his shirt.

Cory was sitting on the front porch, and through the screen Emma could see him staring out at the yard, which was aglow with fireflies.

"That boy is his pride and joy," Mrs. Gamble said, washing the dishes while Emma dried. "Like to killed him when Brenda walked out. Course I didn't know either of them very well then, but soon as he got custody of Mike he hired me. That Brenda." She shook her head. "How she can desert her little boy like that is beyond me. Best thing for Mike would be a mama along with his dad."

"So she doesn't see him much?" Emma said, remembering what Joel had told her.

Mrs. Gamble shook her head again somberly. "No. And

what a shame. She was such a nice little girl from what I hear. And comes from a real good family." She began wiping the counter with the dishcloth. "We're done here now, honey. Why don't you go enjoy the evening?"

Emma thanked her and wandered out to the porch. Joel had said he'd walk her home as soon as he and Mike were done.

She sat down next to Cory and nudged him gently with her elbow. "So, how are you doing?"

"Okay," he said quietly.

She waited, sensing he needed to say something, something that had been troubling him since she got here. She would turn around and find him looking at her, his brows knitted, and then he would look away, flushing. She had intended to sit him down before now, but when Joel was in the hospital there was too much going on.

"Em," he began hesitantly, his hands clutching his knees.

"What is it, Cory?" she asked.

"Is Mom real mad at me?"

"No, of course not, honey. Why?"

"Because of what I did—you know—stealing stuff. I know Joel told you about it."

"She wasn't mad," Emma assured him. "I was there when Joel called."

"So why hasn't she said anything about it when she's called?" Cory burst out. "It's like she's so mad she can't even talk about it."

So that was it. Sunny hadn't brought up the stealing. "Cory," Emma said carefully. "I think that maybe she knows how hard it is to talk about something bothering you so much on the phone. She's waiting to be with you in person so you can work it out together."

"Em, you don't think she'd tell me I can't come back home, do you?" he asked worriedly.

"No, no, Cory. Never. Your mom loves you very much." She reached over and put an arm around his shoulder, drawing him into a hug. "You may not think so because she's been so busy with the new baby, but she needs you now, Cory."

"She does?"

Emma nodded. "She sure does. She's feeling pretty alone herself right now, what with your dad gone. Believe me, Cory. If she didn't have you, she'd fall apart."

Covertly she watched him assimilate this information, and the frown slowly disappeared from his face. He was silent a moment and then, without looking at her, he ducked his head and said, "Thanks, Em," in a tight voice.

We all need to be needed, she thought. Pensively, she glanced up at the porch roof, as if she could see the lighted room above where Joel and his son worked out their pain together.

CHAPTER EIGHT

"You have a visitor," Mrs. Grundy said the next morning from the kitchen door, and Emma looked over her shoulder from the sink where she was washing her breakfast dishes. Clearly Mrs. Grundy was not entirely approving of Emma's comings and goings. She had been waiting up last night when Joel walked Emma home, and she had stood in the hall, arms crossed over her meager chest, frowning as Joel gave Emma a chaste kiss on the forehead.

Joel was standing at the front door when Emma got there, his hands in his pockets and his gaze fixed on the distance. He turned around when he heard her, and she saw that his smile was drawn. She wanted to throw her arms around him, but she waited.

"You aren't out crabbing?" she asked hesitantly.

He shook his head. "Motor that drives the winch went bad, and I had to talk Harold at the marina into working on it for me. He just called, and I was on my way down there." He looked away again. "I thought maybe you'd go out on the water with me today."

Something was wrong. She could see it on his face. But he wasn't going to tell her yet.

"All right," she said. "Let me grab a sweater." It was already hot for early morning, but she knew the water would be much cooler. He still wouldn't quite meet her eyes when he helped her into the pickup truck, and he didn't speak during the ride to the dock.

They were on the water, the wind in their hair, before

she saw the taut set of his shoulder muscles relax. His voice had been brusque and strained when he'd paid Harold for the motor work, and she'd sat silently on the box in front of the cabin until they were underway. Joel's boat, the *Wind Song*, was about the same size as Dave's, but it was evident that he kept it in far better repair. The deck was clean and all the tackle gleamed. In the cabin, matching red blankets were tucked neatly into the two single beds. He had seen her looking at them when they came aboard, but he didn't say anything.

Now he began baiting crab pots and tossing them overboard, a red plastic floating marker at the end of his line. "Mostly Jimmies here on a river bar now," he said almost to himself. "They're looking for the sooks. Blue crabs are different than some other species. The Jimmy will find a female about to molt and he'll pick her up and cradle-carry her with him until she begins to shed her shell. After molting, they mate, sometimes for six to twelve hours. He doesn't abandon her then, because she'd be defenseless without a shell. He continues to carry her another two or three days until her new shell hardens and she can defend herself." He stopped working a minute to wipe his brow and reposition his green cap on his head, and Emma came to stand by his side, leaning her forearms on the boat and staring down into the water. "You'd think people would have as much sense as a fool crab," he said. "You don't desert someone just because it isn't convenient to stick around." She knew now what was bothering him, and she wondered when he had talked to Brenda. It must have been after he walked her home last night. Still, she waited for him to get to the heart of the matter.

"Do you do this year round?" she asked finally, after he'd been silent a long time.

"No. The season's over in the winter. Lots of us go oystering then. You almost have to, to make ends meet."

"What's that like?"

"About like crabbing," he told her, "only colder. I sign on with one of the skipjack crews. They use sails to power the boat while it drags a dredge over the oyster beds." He shook his head. "It was a bad year last year. Seems to go in cycles. Nobody knows why there'll be oysters one year and none the next."

"The ferryman who brought me to the island—Hiram something—said he used to go *'arstering'* as he called it."

"Hiram Bender," Joel said, smiling a bit. "Yeah, when I was a little kid he'd let me go on his boat with my dad. I thought it was great adventure in those days, sleeping onboard and all that stuff. He and Dad would sit around with the rest of the crew at night and tell stories about the Bay. It was something to hear." He was still baiting pots in methodical fashion and tossing them overboard, nudging the boat ahead slowly as he played out the line. "It gets in your blood," he said quietly. "You have these big dreams of moving to the mainland and doing something important with your life, and then when you do go there you find you can't get the Chesapeake out of your system. You think, what's so important about punching a time clock anyway? Or wearing a suit to work every day? None of that matters to a blue crab, and you start to thinking how unimportant it all is, the rest of the world outside the Chesapeake."

"You went away then?" she asked, trying to picture him anywhere but on the water, and not succeeding.

He nodded. "For Brenda. She didn't want to be a waterman's wife, so I went to the mainland with her after Mike was born and tried to be a paper pusher. I think it was mostly her daddy's doing. He made her unhappy with Thorn Haven."

"You must have hated the mainland," she said, reading the distaste in his eyes, still fresh after all this time.

"Yeah. I stuck it out for two years, because she seemed to like it so much better. But I couldn't hack it after a while. All that stupid bull in office politics. It left a bad taste in my mouth. I gotta give Brenda credit for bringing us back here. She knew I was miserable and I guessed she missed her parents some. So we moved back to Thorn Haven and I bought myself a boat and went back to crabbing." He stopped for a moment and stared down at the water. "I don't know. I think Brenda always thought that the accident wouldn't have happened if we'd stayed on the mainland. She never came out and said it, but I could feel it between us. Sometimes when she looked at me . . . I saw it in her eyes."

Emma could understand what he had gone through. She had seen the same silent disappointment and discontent in Paul's eyes whenever she told him they should sell the store. She knew she made him unhappy by bringing it up, but she couldn't stop herself. There wasn't enough money or time to make it work. And it stood between them like a stone wall, effectively cutting off any tender words that might have healed the wounds.

"I know," she said softly, bringing her hand to rest on his on the railing.

His hand turned over and clasped hers. "I think that hurt more than anything, that she thought I could ever do anything to hurt her or Mike. Hell, if it meant that accident not happening I would have sold my soul to that damn office on the mainland."

"The hardest things to accept are the ones where no

one's to blame," Emma said. "Things just go wrong some-times."

"Yeah." He took a deep breath and straightened. "You want some coffee and a sandwich?"

"Sounds fine."

They sat together on a soft brown blanket, leaning against the cabin wall as they ate and drank in silence. "So I guess you're wondering why I'm on such a downer today," he said at length, crumpling his wax paper and tossing it into the open cooler on deck.

She shook her head. "I figure Brenda has something to do with it."

He smiled grimly. "Yeah, she does. She called last night after I got back home. Mike's been wanting to talk to her, to tell her about the camp and Cory. I told her to wait a minute, and she kept saying she had to go. And I said *just one minute for your son.* I went upstairs to get him, and it took him a few minutes to get down the stairs, he was so ex-cited. And damned if she hadn't hung up. Couldn't even face her son on the telephone."

Emma ached; she hated seeing them hurt like that. But Joel had given her no doors to his life, only windows.

" 'No big deal, Dad,' he says to me afterward, like I'm not going to see how disappointed he is, how his eyes are glistening."

"Joel," she said softly, reaching out to touch his tense jaw with her hand because she couldn't listen and not touch him anymore. "Don't make it harder on yourself."

"I can't help it, Emma. It's a damn, crying shame and I can't do a single thing about it."

She could see the tears in his eyes, and he lowered his head and quickly wiped the back of his hand across his face. Then his hand sought Emma's and clasped it tightly. "I shouldn't have brought you out here this morning and dumped all this on you," he said apologetically.

"No," she said quickly. "No, I'm glad you did."

They sat there silently for a while and he held her hand in his rough, callused one, resting them on his upraised knee. "I used to drive him to the hospital for therapy after the accident," he said at length. "Brenda would start to go with us, would comb her hair and get her purse, and then she'd just start crying. Mike would hug her, but she wouldn't stop. And she couldn't look at him." He took a deep breath and squeezed his eyes shut. "Finally, I'd nod to Mike and we'd go out to the car and leave without her. When we got back home she'd be cooking something in the kitchen and smiling and acting like nothing had happened. After the divorce I tried to tell Mike that his mother loved him, but she couldn't stand to see him hurt. I didn't know if I'd reached him or not, and then one day out of the blue he said, 'Mom hates these braces. That's why she can't see me.' And that seems to be how he's handling it. His mother loves him, but she hates the braces."

"He's a strong little boy," Emma said. "You've had a lot to do with that."

Joel shook his head slowly, his eyes so sad and tired when he opened them. "It makes me feel so . . . damn help-less. A kid will do that to you. They want something, and you'd do anything to get it for them, only it's impossible. And you can't bring yourself to tell them that. He's going to have those braces for the rest of his life, and I don't think he has any idea how hard that's going to be." His voice trem-bled, and Emma felt the tears gathering in her throat as she tried to swallow the ache rising there.

"Joel," she whispered brokenly, reaching for him. She came to her knees on the blanket, both arms going around his neck, her mouth exhaling shaky bursts of air against his shoulder. His hand moved to her back and stroked urgent circles there.

"Shhh," he whispered into her hair. "It's okay." And she realized she was crying, her tears wetting his neck. She wiped at them with one hand and groaned. "Emma," he murmured distractedly. "Emma . . ."

"I need you," she whispered brokenly, meaning everything the word implied. She needed this man in her life. She needed to share his pain and his laughter. And she needed him to make love to her, to love away that aching hollow that never left her.

"Don't, Emma," he said, his hand stiffening on her back, his other one smoothing the hair from her forehead. "Don't say that. I didn't mean . . . I didn't bring you out here to do this to you."

"I know," she said fervently. "But it doesn't matter. I need you now, Joel."

She could hear the barely disguised anguish of his own need in his voice, now husky with tension. "Oh, God, Emma. I can't be strong for both of us. Don't do this, because I want you so bad I don't think I can stop." He was rubbing his cheek over her hair, and she could feel the wanting trembling inside him.

But she didn't want him to stop. She needed his quiet strength, and she needed his arms around her. She needed to take him inside her and bring to life the long dormant emotions she'd buried. She'd never experienced such urgency before, as if she'd die if he didn't hold her and kiss her. She curved her hand around his rough jaw and stroked, her thumb finding his lower lip, smooth and solid as metal, and sliding along it, brushing over and over until he let his breath out with a moan.

"Emma," he ground out, his voice laden with the pent-up force of the storm that had nearly killed them that day. But this was a storm of a different kind. This was heat and hunger and burning need, and it had burgeoned into a fierce flame that scorched them both.

His hands found her waist and pulled the lavender short-sleeved blouse free of her jeans. His fingers trembled as they stole their way upward under the blouse. Emma was trembling, too, all over, inside and out. Her head still rested on his shoulder, and now he brought his mouth down to her ear and from there to the column of her throat, leaving an incendiary trail of sensation. His mouth sought hers as his fingers touched her swelling breasts through the thin fabric of her bra, and Emma's head came up with a groan, her lips meeting his in unrestrained greed. *How was it possible to feel so much?* she wondered briefly. She felt as though she had been dead inside a long time, and now those bitter ashes of numbness were scraped away, revealing a molten core of feeling.

He devoured her with his fingers and his mouth, each touch bringing her to a higher pitch of passion. His hands slid to her waist, his mouth leaving hers long enough for him to bring her around and lay her backward against his raised knee. He framed her face with his hands as he smiled down at her shakily. "You are so beautiful," he said slowly. "I've wanted you for such a long time now."

"Make love to me," she murmured, staring up into rapturous green eyes, as brilliant as emerald fire and as captivating. His expression held her in sway, as though she were too precious to touch and yet too precious to ever let go. Glistening drops of salt water clung to his black hair, and the breeze touched them and made them sparkle in the sun. *He was like a pagan god risen from the sea,* Emma thought, *so strong and vital.*

Joel's fingers fumbled with the buttons of her blouse, and he couldn't seem to stop looking into her face, a tenderness approaching awe in his eyes. "Why are these damn buttons so tiny?" he finally demanded in exasperation, smiling crookedly.

Emma's fingers touched his, and suddenly she was as fumble-fingered as he was. "I think they shrank," she murmured, a whispery laugh bubbling past her lips.

His fingers played with the buttons, then moved to her breasts, teasing them through the blouse, and Emma's breath ebbed away. He replaced his hand with his mouth, his tongue moving languidly over the clothclad nipple until she moaned. When he raised his head the wet fabric cooled in the breeze, and her nipple tightened against it. He went to work on the buttons again and then helped her shrug out of the blouse. Her lacy bra followed and she lay before him, naked from the waist up. The sun shone on her with lazy warmth, and the breeze dallied over her bare flesh. She felt full and ripe and ready for her lover.

Emma caressed his hard chest and ribs through the blue cotton work-shirt he'd rolled up over his elbows. She began working on his buttons, her work impeded considerably by his penchant for lowering his mouth to her breasts every few seconds. She kept forgetting what she was doing, and she knew she was watching his face through glazed eyes. By some miracle she got his shirt off him and sighed throatily as she stared at the hard patchwork of muscles, dark hair a sparse thatch between flat male nipples, then thickening as it feathered down to his stomach and disappeared lower. Emma had always been a deliberate woman, not coy, and now she looked at him openly. Her eyes slowly moved upward, drinking in the sight of him, and when they settled at last on his face he gave her a crooked smile. "Touch me,

Emma," he whispered. "I want to feel your hands on me."

She needed no other invitation. Her palms grazed his chest, pressing flat circles on his nipples, and then her hands glided lower, fingers circling sensuously in the dark hair, then weaving across to his ribs and finally back to that springy dark hair. She touched him as a lover, a woman who wanted to know the mysteries of this man's body and yearned to give up her own secrets in turn. Her fingers lightly grazed here, flicked with her nails there on his ribs, playfully skimmed just past his jeans. A deep groan issued from Joel. "Lord, Kendrick, you're driving me out of my mind."

She smiled, and when he reached for his belt said, "No, let me." She skimmed off the belt, then slid to her knees while he kicked off his shoes. She tugged on his jeans after she had avidly teased him by unzipping the zipper so slowly that his breathing became labored. When she had dispensed with his jeans and underwear, she simply looked at him again, her blood thickened with desire. *Yes, yes, yes,* thrummed her heart.

"I'd carry you to bed in the cabin," he whispered, "but I don't think I can make it that far, honey. You seem to have turned my legs to jelly."

Still smiling seductively, she began to unfasten her jeans, but he shook his head, a devilish gleam in his eyes. "Oh, no you don't, Emma. My turn." He reached for her waist and pulled her down onto his lap again.

"Your leg," she murmured, worried, but he shook his head.

"It doesn't hurt," he assured her. Then he went to work on her jeans, his fingers exploring each inch of her flesh as he peeled them off her. He lifted her hips with one hand as he eased the denim fabric down and then his hand slid with tantalizing slowness over the smooth skin of her buttocks and hooked her underpants. Emma had the vague impression that her bones had somehow dissolved, and she was a mass of quivering nerves, each nerve on fire. A moan escaped her as she lay naked on his lap and his hands parted her legs to tenderly explore. Ever so gently he stroked until she twisted on his legs and cried his name.

He lifted her then and turned her so that she lay on top of him, belly to belly, her legs between his. She could feel him, glistening and smooth and ready for her. She ached with the need to feel him inside her.

"Oh, Joel," she murmured. "I . . . want you so much."

"I want to make it good for you," he whispered. "I've made love to you a hundred times in my head and now I can hardly think straight." His hands moved down her back to her hips and lifted her slightly. As he lowered her, she felt him enter her, and it was the most exquisite thrusting pleasure. He rocked her slowly, and her breath hissed through her throat with each intimate touch of him inside her.

She was lying on his chest, her arms circling his neck, but now he put his hands on her ribs and gently raised her. She didn't know what he was going to do until he lowered his head and his tongue touched her nipple. "Oh," she gasped.

He continued slowly thrusting into her as his lips sucked her breast, drawing the creamy softness into his mouth and then letting the breeze play over her naked, moist flesh. Emma's nipples hardened in rapture and his tongue flicked them, making her moan with pleasure. She had never known such lovemaking existed. She had never been loved like this before. It was intoxicating and addictive. Each pleasure he gave her bound her more closely to him.

The boat moved gently beneath them, as though the whole world was caught in the rhythm of their lovemaking. She could feel the sun bathing her back with a blazing warmth, but even the sun couldn't compare to the heat building inside Emma.

Joel groaned and brought his mouth to her own, kissing her deeply and with a hunger that left no doubt in Emma's mind that he truly had wanted her for a long time. Her body was still poised above him and now he slowly lowered her to rest on him as his thrusts grew more urgent. His hands slid to her hips and held them still as he moved inside her, and Emma arched her belly against his, glistening flesh sliding over glistening flesh.

Their breath came in hard gasps and as Emma felt the pleasure building to an undeniable force she looked into her lover's face. And she saw a man she loved and wanted with her always. He was watching her with rapt attention, the sight of her a spur to his own passion, and now he buried his face in her hair and murmured, "My beautiful, brave Emma . . . I need you so."

She had seen everything she ever wanted in his eyes, and she gave a hoarse cry as the sweet promises of his hard body bore her into a fiery region of sensation. Wave after wave of sensual pleasure pulsed through her, leaving her weak and shivering.

"Emma," he whispered softly, his rough legs wrapping around her possessively. His hand trembled as he brushed back her hair. "There, honey," he soothed her, kissing her damp neck.

"I love you, Joel," she murmured as she drifted toward the edge of a drugged sleep. She was hovering there in the darkness behind her closed lids, awash in the last remnants of physical release, but still she felt the pain inside him at what she'd said. It was in the involuntary stiffening of his body and the way his hand stilled in her hair. She opened her eyes, his name on her lips.

"Don't say anything," he said, shaking his head gently. He lowered her to the blanket at his side and smoothed her hair, looking into her face a long time. "The minister's daughter is such an amazing woman," he told her whimsically.

"I really do love you," she insisted.

Joel's smile was sad. "No, Emma, don't say that. You give love so beautifully. But I can't take it."

"What about me?" she asked, locking gazes with him. "Tell me how you feel about me, Joel."

"If things were different . . ." He turned his head, but not before she'd seen the stark loneliness in his eyes and the flicker—more than a flicker, the flame—of what she meant to him. And Emma was content then to close her eyes and rest her head on his shoulders. Because she knew how he felt.

It was early afternoon when she woke. He had covered her with the blanket and put her sweater under her head. She turned her head to look at him, enjoying watching him when he didn't know she was. He was rhythmically baiting crab pots and tossing them overboard, his leg nudging the boat's controls to move it gently ahead with each new pot. He was all beauty and fluid motion, and she drank in the sight of him. A lock of black hair fell rakishly over his forehead, and the shadowy beard on his jaw emphasized the deep green of his eyes.

He glanced over his shoulder and caught her looking at him. A slow smile spread over his face. "Why are you looking at me like that?" he said, grinning foolishly.

She just grinned back, and a moment later he apparently decided she was more interesting than the crab pots, because he idled the engine and came to sit on the blanket beside her, pulling off his heavy gloves.

He lifted the edge of the blanket and gave her a mischievous waggle of his brows before his hand crept beneath the coarse fabric and found her back. He stroked down and over her hip tenderly, his eyes intent on her face.

"You know," he said, introducing the topic again, "you shouldn't look at me like that."

"Like what?" she said, curving her body into the sweep of his hand.

"Like you think maybe I'll come back and crawl under that blanket with you." His grin broadened, and his hand continued its explorations.

Emma held up the edge of the blanket and did her own imitation of eyebrow waggling. His grin broadened and his fingers began undoing his shirt. "I'm so easy," he teased her.

A minute later his clothes were discarded and he was holding her against his hard flesh. "Emma, Emma," he breathed into her hair. "What am I going to do with you?"

The question was half teasing, half heartache, but neither had time to answer it as his mouth found hers and he groaned. She was ready for him the instant he touched her, and she twined her arms and legs around him to hold him tight. God, she loved the feel of him. He was such a big rough man when he was working, but with her he was all gentleness and tender passion.

His fingers caressed her urgently, down her hips and over the softness of her inner thighs, making her gasp with pleasure as he touched her intimately. His lips roving over her mouth and neck, he used his fingers to fuel the fire that burned in her loins, bringing her to the edge again.

"I want you," she whispered raggedly, her hands kneading his firm back. "Joel . . . come to me." She was claiming him as lover, and though she knew he would try to keep his heart from her, she would have him for those long, mindless moments when his body became one with hers.

"Emma." The one word was filled with all that he didn't say, and he entered her possessively, making love to her with the hunger of a man who wanted her so badly. Emma felt the familiar spiral of pleasure that weakened her knees and wrung a heart-stopping response from her very soul. She would give this man anything . . .

"We have to go now," he said afterward, his eyes shadowy as he smoothed the hair from her face. "It's getting late."

He didn't look at her as he began putting his clothes on, and she let her eyes linger on his beautiful shape, watching the powerful muscles move. He was pulling on his pants, and the jagged scar on his leg stood in stark relief against his bronze skin. She thought of that desperate night alone on the island and how he had protected her then. He was trying to protect her now, too, trying not to hurt her by loving her. And Emma wanted that love. Smiling sadly, she found her underwear and slowly dragged it on.

They hardly spoke as they rode back to the dock, the misty breeze dampening their hair and faces. The sun burned through a layer of filmy clouds, and Emma felt a thin crease of perspiration building down her back. The heat was the kind that clung to the skin and made clothes stick like damp paper.

"I want to show you something," he said as they got into the truck and she sat back and waited until he took a narrow dirt road that ran along the Bay. He pulled up to a large wooden building with only a few windows and some kind of vent pipes on the roof. She got out of the truck and followed him to a steel door at the front.

"Hey, Flint," Joel said, poking his head inside what Emma saw was an office. "You busy?"

"Naw, Joel," the big man behind the desk said, grinning. Emma saw that he was dressed in jeans. "You bring me a good load of Jimmies today?"

"Afraid not. Just got my boat working again this morning, so I set some pots. Listen, Flint, this is a friend of mine, Emma Kendrick. She's from Iowa, and I was wondering if I could take her around back and show her the picking room."

"Yeah, sure." Flint nodded to Emma and smiled. "Go on ahead. And bring me some Jimmies tomorrow," he called after Joel.

"This is a packing plant," Joel told Emma as he led her around the side of the building. "The crabs are cooked whole in huge steam kettles. Then they go to the picking room." He came to a screen door at the side of the building, and Emma heard a din of women's voices, laughter, and a steady thumping. "This is where my mom used to work," Joel said, pushing open the screen door. Emma followed him in, noting that the voices immediately stopped talking and laughing, and a curious silence ensued. About thirty-five women sat around a huge stainless-steel table filled with cooked crabs. Each woman had a small curved knife poised in her hand, and Emma saw that each had small bandages on her fingers.

"Well, if it ain't Buckshot Rivers," drawled a big black woman sitting near some kind of window where crabs continued to empty onto the table. She wiped her hand on her apron and gave him a toothy smile. "How you doin', honey?"

"Fine, Mary." He put his arm around Emma's waist and pulled her forward. "This is Emma Kendrick. Her nephew's at the football camp, so I brought her by to see the best crab pickers in the world."

The woman hooted. "More talkin' than pickin' going on at the moment," Mary said, shooting an assessing glance around the table.

"Show us how you do it, Mary," someone called, and soon a chorus of encouragement went around the table. "C'mon, Mary!"

Mary looked at everyone over the top of her black-rimmed glasses, then wiped her hands again. "Someone got a stopwatch?" she said.

"Here!" a girl called. "My watch has one on it." She passed the watch forward to Joel, and he checked it.

"All right," he said. "Tell me when you're ready, Mary."

The older woman eyed the crabs in front of her and cleared herself a work space. She took the knife in one hand and nodded to Joel. "Go!" he said, and the room erupted in whoops as the women cheered on Mary.

Emma couldn't believe how quickly the woman's hands moved. It was almost a blur, and try as she might Emma couldn't follow Mary's movements. The woman's fingers flew as she extracted the meat from one crab and then another and packed it into a round blue can in front of her, neatly discarding the shells to the side of the table. The cheers grew louder as the can was nearly filled, and when the meat reached the top Mary held her hands up in the air. The women were shouting and applauding, and Joel clicked the watch in his hand.

"One pound in three minutes, ten seconds," he said, shaking his head. "Pretty near a new record, Mary."

Mary shrugged and calmly went about cracking open the

next crab, but Emma could see the light shining in the woman's eyes. "I don't know how you can work so fast," Emma said in wonder, and Mary beamed.

"Been doin' it a lot of years," she said.

"Mary was runner-up at Crisfield ten years ago," Joel told Emma. "They have a crab derby and a picking contest every year."

"You tell your friend about your mama's crab in the derby?" Mary asked, and Joel smiled.

"No, ma'am. Not yet."

Mary went on picking crabs, but she grinned at Emma slyly. "This one was just a little bigger than a turd then," she said, pointing the knife at Joel. "And his mama decided she was goin' to enter a crab in the Crisfield Derby. So she tells Joel's daddy to get her the biggest, fastest crab in the Bay for that race. And I says, 'Laura Ann, you ain't gonna win nohow.' But she says, 'Oh, yes, I am, Mary. You just watch.' And then here comes little Joel with this big ole Jimmy he caught with a piece of twine and some bull lips from the butcher for bait." She tossed aside a crab shell and winked at Emma. "And that boy says he's gonna enter his crab, too. Well, Laura Ann liked to have a fit. She got her crab and named it Flash and she be feedin' it fresh shrimp and anything nice like that. And Joel he got his crab and be feedin' it any trashy stuff he can find and bringing it into the garage to run practice races. And he calls his Tornado. And on Derby Day in Crisfield, damned if both those crabs don't win their own heats and go up against each other in the big race. I recollect as Laura Ann's crab was number one hundred twenty-two and little Joel's was ninety-eight. So the race gets goin' and all these crabs are out on that wet metal track goin' ever' which way. And then, Lord, here comes Laura Ann's crab and it looks like it's gonna win that race. It's almost to the finish line and durned if Joel's crab don't up and grab holt of Flash and turn that crab around the wrong way. So off goes Flash backwards and Tornado is right behind and some other Jimmy goes and wins that race."

Joel was laughing and scratching his eye with one finger as he listened. "Mama sure was put out about my crab," he said, shaking his head and laughing some more.

"Make no mistake about that," Mary confirmed. She winked at Emma again. "She says to that boy of hers, 'Joel Rivers, how on earth did you come to get such a mean, ornery crab that it went and kept my crab from winnin'?' And he says, 'Don't rightly know, Mama. He got a bit contrary last Friday after I raced him in the garage. Musta been that buckshot he ate.' And Mary she says, 'Buckshot?' And Joel says, 'Yeah, I thought it would make him faster so I mixed it up with peanut butter.' And the folks standin' around heard and they got to laughing and next thing you know Joel's being called Buckshot. But you know what?" She stopped working to fix her bright brown eyes on Emma. "The next year that boy went out and brought home a big old Jimmy for his mama and that crab won second place in the Crisfield Derby. I asked her if she'd been feedin' that Jimmy buckshot, but she wouldn't tell me." She chuckled deeply, resting her hands on her ample lap. "No, weren't many like Laura Ann. Lordy, I miss her."

When Emma looked at Joel she saw that his face was filled with a gentle sadness, and his eyes had darkened to a murky green. "Well, we'd better be going, and let you get back to work. Thanks for showing Emma how to pick crabs."

"Anytime, honey," Mary called, waving her knife at them as they went back out the screen door. The chatter and laughter inside the picking room increased as they left, and Emma could hear the women's voices all the way to the truck. There was a rhythm and a music to the sound, punctuated by the falling crab shells. The outside air was even more stifling than in the picking room, and Emma wiped her hand over her upper lip.

"So that's how you came to be called Buckshot," she said when they were on the road again. "And here I worried that you'd killed someone."

He gave her a sideways glance and a half-smile. "Oh, you did, did you?"

"Mmm-hmm. And I thought you were some kind of brawling tough guy who had kidnapped my nephew."

"You wouldn't have been far wrong at one time," he said, giving her a quick look.

Emma turned to watch him, seeing a brooding restlessness settle on his face. "What happened?" she asked.

"It was after Mom had her breakdown," he said, slowing the truck and pulling it to the shoulder of the road. He sat for a minute with his forearms resting on top of the steering wheel, his eyes fixed on some point outside the truck. "She was in a hospital on the mainland," he said. "Dad was still working sunup to sundown on the boat, so I was pretty much on my own. I was a kid, but I guess I thought I was pretty tough. I started running with a rough crowd, some kids who lived on the mainland and didn't do much of anything except think up ways to get beer and get drunk on their butts." His brows drew together. "Mom got out of the hospital, and I stayed around home more, but I wasn't doing my schoolwork and it looked like I might flunk. Money was short, so Dad put me to work on an oyster dredger. And then Mom died. She was all worn out and she got pneumonia that winter . . ."

"That must have been rough on you," Emma said softly.

A shadow of the boy he used to be flashed across his face as he looked at Emma, and she saw stoic pride and flinty self-reliance. "It was worse on Dad," he said flatly, averting his head again. "He stayed out on the water longer and longer hours, and I got wild again. Almost got myself arrested once after I tied one on and broke a store window downtown." The tense set of his shoulders relaxed some and he gave a humorless smile. "Mary came down to the police station and got me. Took me home with her, too. She has a big son, Wendell." He laughed. "Wendell took me under his wing and gave Mary his promise that I wouldn't get in trouble again. He about broke my jaw a couple of times, but he kept that promise. They got me back in school and kept me so busy with chores when I wasn't studying that there wasn't any time to get in trouble. Mary got me a part-time job as a stockboy in the grocery store, and then made me go to the junior college." He nodded slowly. "She pushed my ass, Kendrick. She made me do things when I didn't care about anything anymore. That lady's more than just a champion crab picker. She's a whole lot more," he finished softly. "I was one lucky kid."

"You were," Emma agreed quietly. It was obvious, too, how much Mary had cared about Joel's mother, Laura Ann.

He glanced at the rearview mirror, then pulled the truck back onto the road. "Dad was never the same. He wandered around the coast working boats here and there, drinking himself blind on weekends. He died a few years ago in Virginia." He was silent a long time, and Emma stared out the window. "That crab picking plant I took you to," he said slowly. "That was the only job my mom could get. That was the kind of life she had."

Emma knew what he was telling her. That was the only life he could offer her, and they both knew it.

CHAPTER NINE

"I don't understand this," Emma said, eyeing Cory and Mike suspiciously. "Now tell me one more time why I'm driving you two to this fair."

"Be-cause," Cory said with ten-year-old male logic, and he and Mike burst into fresh giggles. "Joel can't take us, Mrs. Gamble hates fairs, and you weren't doing anything."

"That makes me feel *so* good," she assured him as she maneuvered the car from the ferry and waved goodbye to Hiram Bender. "What kind of fair did you say this is?"

A fresh spate of giggles was all the answer she got, and Emma resigned herself to a long day. It had been three weeks since she and Joel made love on his boat, and he had been careful not to touch her since then. But often she caught him looking at her with a brooding intensity.

The grounds where the boys told her to turn bore a long white banner fluttering between two wooden posts, a banner that said something about a tournament. Emma was beginning to smell a rat, and the boys were giggling again. She parked the car and watched as Cory grasped Mike's arms and helped him slide from the car seat. The boys were so close that Emma knew they would be lifelong friends, no matter how far apart they were.

They seemed to be looking for something, and Emma trailed behind them, soaking up the atmosphere. This was apparently some kind of medieval fair reenactment, complete with strolling minstrels in costume, lute players, and various food booths offering delicacies from fruit to good old futuristic frozen yogurt. The boys made her get them each a chocolate yogurt cone, and Emma dabbed at a drop she spilled on her red-checked blouse. Her jeans were already dusty from the clouds that rose wherever people walked.

"Come on, Em, over here," Cory insisted, tugging her along by her shirt. He dragged her to the bleachers and found them a seat on the bottom row, helping Mike to sit down and stow his crutches on the ground.

"What is this?" Emma asked, looking around at the dirt ring in front of them. There was a pole in the middle of the ring and another at the end. The bleachers were filling up and Emma had to raise her voice to be heard.

"It's a jousting tournament," Mike announced, grinning from ear to ear.

Emma looked out at the dirt ring and back at the boy. "A what?"

"A jousting tournament," he repeated gleefully. "It's a big deal in Maryland. You'll see."

A gravelly-voiced announcer welcomed them over the PA system and gave the rules for the next event. While he talked, a man went to each of the two poles in the ring and attached something to them. *Well,* Emma thought, *this was showing some promise of being interesting.* The boys were whispering and pointing at the men on horseback gathering by the ring's gate. *This is some kind of rodeo,* Emma decided.

The first rider was announced, and a bay mare came cantering into the ring. The horse picked up speed, and Emma saw the rider heft a long wooden pole in his right hand. As she watched in fascination, the rider made a pass at the first post in the ring, trying to snare something, and the crowd gave a shout. He rode full tilt at the second post, and this time the crowd groaned in disappointment.

"What's he doing?" Emma demanded, shaking Cory's arm.

"He's trying to get the rings," Cory told her in a voice that was clearly embarrassed by her density. The rings were checked, and the next rider came galloping at them. This guy missed the first ring and hit the post instead, and he went toppling from his perch on the horse's back. Emma gasped along with the crowd, but a second later the man climbed to his feet, waving sheepishly to the bleachers, and everyone applauded.

Emma bent down to retie her sneaker as the next rider was announced, and her head shot up as she recognized the name. *Joel Rivers?* She glanced quickly at the boys and saw them grinning at her. So they were all in this together.

Joel came trotting into the ring on a roan horse, holding up his hand and calling to the announcer. He stopped the horse right in front of the bleachers and dismounted. It was hard to say who was grinning harder, the boys or Joel, and Emma jumped to her feet as he approached her.

"What are you doing on a horse?" she demanded worriedly as he approached her.

"I'm riding," he informed her, grinning as big as you please. "Were you surprised?"

"You're going to get killed," she said, plucking at his sleeve. "You crazy man."

"Was she surprised?" Joel asked the boys, and they giggled in chorus. "Now, here, honey," he said, handing her a white rose. "This is for good luck." He started to leave, but Emma was still grasping his sleeve.

"You're going to fall off that horse and get smashed," she hissed. "You stop this."

"I need a kiss," he informed her, turning back around and tipping her chin up with his hand. The bleacher ob-

144

servers applauded as his lips brushed Emma's, and then he was walking to his horse again. "You just better not fall off that horse," she warned him. As she sat down, the woman behind her clapped her on the shoulder. "Don't worry, honey," she said sympathetically. "The horse knows what it's doing even if your man don't."

Emma clutched her rose and fervently hoped so.

Joel guided his horse back to the gate and Emma closed her eyes. She could hear galloping hooves, then the thud of wood against wood. When she dared open one eye Joel was safely at the other end of the ring, holding aloft his wooden pole and looking cocky and handsome in his jeans and black T-shirt.

"He did it!" Mike was shouting as he rocked backward. "Dad got both rings!"

Emma put her hand on Mike's shoulder to steady him and he grinned at her happily. "Boy, he's something else," Mike crowed.

Emma nodded, dazed. "Your dad's something else all right," she agreed.

This was the first of a series of heats, and Joel was in the finals. Emma couldn't watch then either, but she knew from the shouts around her that he'd done well. He came to sit with them after that, and they all watched the rest of the finals together.

"So what did you think?" he asked, grinning as he put his arm around her shoulders.

"I think you're nuts," she told him levelly. Then she relented. "But you look awfully good on that horse. How come you never told me you could ride a horse?"

"Because I wanted to surprise you," he told her, the grin broadening. "And you were surprised, weren't you?"

"Oh, yes," she assured him. She'd been that all right.

She clutched her rose and stole a sideways glance at him. Her heart swelled with pride and love at the sight of his rugged profile. She touched his hand on her shoulder, intertwining their fingers. He looked at her, and the light in those green eyes was nearly her undoing. Lord, but she loved this man! Any fool could see that they belonged together, any fool except this big horse-riding one beside her who still insisted he couldn't give her a good life. On the spur of the moment she took her free hand and gave him a light punch to the ribs.

"Hey, what's that for?" he asked, mystified.

"That's just for being you, Rivers," she told him, and he grinned at her again.

When they announced that he was the winner, Emma was as excited as he was. He stood, whooping, and picked her up with both arms around her waist, twirling her in a circle despite her feeble protests. He would have carried her all the way to the judging stand if she hadn't made him stop and put her down. When he came back with his ten-inch-high trophy he twirled her all over again. "Stop!" she protested.

"You're not going to get sick, are you?" he asked, grinning.

"Lord, no, but I'm going to thump you again."

"Well, let's go home then," he told her. "There's a party back at my house."

He rode back with her and the boys in her car, and he finally told her that he'd been riding horses since he was a little boy and his mother's father put him on one. And he'd entered his first jousting tournament on a lark and enjoyed it so much he'd done it ever since.

The party was already in progress when they reached the house, and Juice waved from the back of a pickup truck where he was unloading a case of beer. Emma recognized some of the men from the docks, but the women were largely unfamiliar. Joel looped his arm around her shoulders and shepherded her from one person to another, introducing her as Emma Kendrick From Iowa.

"Will you stop?" she finally said as they left yet another group.

"Stop what?"

"Stop introducing me like I'm from a foreign country. Somebody even told me I don't have much of an accent."

He laughed. "All right. Listen, I have to go run an errand. Now you stay here and talk to Fran." He pushed her toward a thin, blond woman in shorts and a halter top. "She'll take good care of you."

"I don't need taking care of," Emma told him, wondering where he was going but too stubborn to ask. Her words were lost on him though as he disappeared around the house toward his truck.

"You must be Emma Kendrick From Iowa," Fran said, holding out her hand. "I'm Juice's friend."

"It's nice to meet you," Emma said, shaking her hand and glancing over her shoulder as the truck roared down the drive, throwing up a cloud of dust.

"Joel says you teach Sunday school," Fran said.

Apparently Joel had passed around her resumé. "My father is a minister," Emma said. "It sort of comes with the territory."

"I teach the class my son's in," Fran said. "Teddy's five."

"That's a tough class," Emma said sympathetically. "They don't like to sit still very long."

"Tell me about it," Fran said. "I've been trying to come up with some kind of lesson plan to hold their interest."

Juice came by with two cold beers for them, winked at Fran and then disappeared. Emma and Fran sat down on the porch steps and Emma brought up several lesson plans she'd used in the past.

She was giving Fran the details of an Old Testament program she particularly liked when she looked up and saw Louis Richter walking toward them.

"Oh, crud," Fran muttered. "What's he doing here?"

"Hello there," Louis said to Emma. He nodded coolly to Fran, and Emma didn't fail to notice the thinly veiled hostility. "Em," he said, and she immediately resented his abbreviated use of her given name. "I was wondering if you wanted one of the team pictures with Cory in it?"

"That would be nice," Emma said shortly.

"Well, great. I could run you out to the office later to pick it up."

"That's all right. I'm sure I could get it sometime."

Louis shifted his weight from one foot to the other, but his oily smile never wavered. "Well, don't wait too long. Only got a couple left." He nodded to her and left, and Emma expelled her breath.

"One thing you can say for him," Fran sniffed. "He heals fast." She gave Emma a significant look. "Joel broke his nose several weeks back."

Emma quickly looked at the retreating figure of Louis and then back to Fran. "So that's who he hit," she said, not disapprovingly.

"Yeah, old Louis was out cold for a good three minutes."

"How come he hit him?"

Fran looked uncomfortable and stared down at her beer a minute. "Well, he was making some remarks about Teddy."

"Your son?"

Fran nodded. "I've never been married, and to someone like Louis Richter that makes me and Teddy fair game for his little attempts at humor. I think Juice was going to hit him, too, but Joel got to him first. Louis threatened a lawsuit, but someone in the bar pointed out that he deserved what he got, and if he sued a lot of other people were liable to take a poke at him, too." Emma took a long swallow of beer and leaned back against the step. Joel's truck was coming up the drive, and she smiled slowly as she watched it.

"Well, would you look at that," Fran said in a low voice as the truck stopped and a woman jumped down gingerly from the passenger side. Joel sat in the truck a moment, and then he got out and smiled at the woman tentatively. He led her away from the party and toward the back of the house, never once looking at Emma, and Emma felt her heart crash into her shoes as she watched the woman beside Joel, her long chestnut hair catching the setting sun. She knew who it was before Fran spoke.

"I'll be damned," Fran said. "It's Brenda. Now how do you suppose Joel got her here?"

Emma didn't know, but it was obvious that Brenda was finally going to see her son. And Emma knew what that meant to Mike—and Joel. If things worked out, then Mike might have his mother back in his life. Maybe Joel was right, Emma thought sadly. There was no life here for her. She couldn't begrudge a sad little boy his mother or a lonely man his ex-wife.

Fran pulled Emma's thoughts back to the porch with a low whistle. "The man's a miracle worker," she said in admiration. "If he could get Brenda back here to visit, I wouldn't be surprised if he could get her to move in."

"That would be wonderful," Emma said, hoping her voice didn't betray her.

"Oh, hey," Fran said, looking at Emma's face. "You got a thing for the guy, don't you? I'm sorry. Running off at the mouth about Brenda like that."

"It's okay," Emma assured her. "Believe me, it's not much of a thing I've got going."

"Well, don't mind me. Say, have you met Juice's sister Joan?" Emma knew that Fran was tactfully changing the subject, but she was grateful not to have to talk about Brenda anymore, and she followed Fran to a knot of women around the picnic table where she listened to stories of children and boyfriends and husbands. Twilight came to the Bay, and stars shone down on the remnants of the party, and still Joel and Brenda hadn't come out of the house.

The men's voices had grown gradually louder as the party progressed and the beer flowed, and now they swapped stories under the cherry tree as the dew gathered on the grass. Fran had gone home to check on Teddy, and Emma had gone to sit on the porch step, away from everyone. She was thinking of walking back to Mrs. Grundy's when Louis appeared in front of her.

"So, you look abandoned," he said.

Emma shrugged. "I was thinking of calling it a night."

"Well, listen, maybe we could run by my office and get that picture. It would just take a minute."

Emma hesitated. Under normal circumstances she didn't want to go anywhere with Louis Richter, and tonight her mood was worse than usual.

"I've got to go out of town for a few days," he said, "and I kind of wanted to get Cory's jacket back to him, too. He, uh, left it when he moved out of the dorm."

"All right," Emma said in resignation. If that was Cory's new denim jacket, Sunny would kill him for coming home without it. She knew Louis was trying to finagle another

150

date with her, but she was beyond caring at this point. At the moment she didn't like herself very much, because she kept hoping that Brenda would go back home where she belonged.

She was silent on the ride to Louis's office in his sporty little car, and he kept clearing his voice and looking at her sideways.

"Football field's dark now," he noted needlessly when he parked in the lot by the wire fence. They entered a low brick building, their footsteps echoing through the hall until Louis stopped to unlock an office door. "This is the elementary school," he told her. "We talked them into building the field, though, and now we can run the camp every summer."

"It's nice," Emma said in distraction.

"Yeah," Louis agreed. He took Cory's jacket from a peg behind the door and handed it to her, then got one of the large black and white pictures from his desk drawer. "Here. The kids were all excited getting their picture taken. Could hardly get them to sit still."

Emma smiled as she looked down at the picture in her hands, all the boys grinning broadly, Mike sitting in front with his score book, his crutches under the bench. "They'll never forget this summer," she said, meaning it.

"Yeah . . ." Louis's voice trailed off, and he sat on the edge of his desk, staring down at the floor. "Listen, you have something going with Rivers, don't you?"

Emma's temper flared. "I wish people would stop saying that!" she snapped.

"All I meant was you aren't, well, available?" he asked, scratching his head awkwardly.

Emma sighed. She was bewildered, tired, and confused. Available? Probably that, too. "No," she said wearily, shaking her head. "I'm sorry. I'm just not interested in starting a relationship right now." God, that sounded prim.

"Not with me, anyway," he said.

"Not with anyone," she said, venting her true feelings of the moment. "Not now."

"Okay, I understand," he said, rising and jingling his keys. He led her back out the building and to his car. "Rivers is an okay guy," he told her as he started the engine. "Got a bit of a bad break with his kid. He and I mixed it up a bit one day, but he's all right. Saw him with his ex-wife tonight." He pulled out onto the road, and Emma remained silent. "Well, I wish him nothing but the best of luck," he said. "That kid needs a mother around."

Emma caught her lower lip in her teeth and stared out the window. It was dark now, and reflections of the moon danced on the Bay. This day had started so well and ended on such a melancholy note. It surprised Emma as they pulled into Joel's drive to note that the party was over and there was no one about. It surprised her even more to realize she hoped Brenda hadn't disappointed Mike and Joel.

"Thank you," she said to Louis, motioning him back when he would have gotten out of the car and seen her to the door. "Good night." She stood there while he drove off and then went to her car. Feeling foolish, she remembered she had left her purse and keys inside Joel's house. She would have to go in unless she wanted to brave Mrs. Grundy's icy stare as she unlocked the door for her yet another time. Emma wavered and then chose Joel's dark house as the lesser of two evils.

She had left the purse in the kitchen, so she went around the back, finding the steps by the light of the moon. She opened the screen, went in and softly closed it behind her. She couldn't find the wall switch by feel, so she fumbled in the dark, making her way to the table.

"You here to steal the silverware?" came Joel's voice in the dark, and Emma jumped violently, hitting her shin on a chair.

"Ow!" she cried. "You scared me half to death!"

A switch clicked and the small brass lamp on the oak hutch came on, casting a light as pale as the moonlight on the Bay. Joel was sitting at the kitchen table by the hutch, his chair tilted back on two legs. He was watching her, and he didn't look happy. Emma rubbed her shin and glared at him.

"So, did you and Louis have a good time?" he asked, obviously in a mood to argue.

"We went to get Cory's jacket and his football picture," she said irritably, realizing she'd tossed the things into her car already, so her excuse looked flimsy. Not that she owed Joel an explanation anyway. "And how did you know I was with Louis?"

"Juice saw you leave."

"It must be nice to have a dependable spy network," she grumbled.

"I was worried half sick about you, you know," he said in an aggrieved tone.

"Well, I can't imagine why."

"You're with Louis and you can't imagine why I'd worry?" he asked dryly.

"As I recall, you're the one who fixed me up with him in the first place. I should think you'd be proud of your matchmaking abilities." She was just as aggravated as he was, and she wasn't averse to letting him know it.

"Yeah, but I thought you'd have more sense than to go anywhere with him again."

"Well, maybe I don't have such good sense about who

153

I'm seen with," Emma snapped, grabbing at her purse on the floor. "I seem to hang around with you a lot."

"Hey, come here," he said in the silence that followed.

"Why? Do you want to insult my good sense some more?"

"No. I want you to come over here closer. I had a rough day."

She put her purse back down and went, still irritated. He put his arm around her waist and rested his head against the flat part of her stomach. "You want to take a walk?" he asked.

"No," she said, still not letting go of her bad mood.

"Come on," he said, standing up and pulling her toward the door. He held her hand in his, and she trailed along beside him, not saying anything and not looking at him. *So where do we stand?* she wondered. *Am I your friend or your lover or what?*

They walked down by the edge of the water in back of the house, and Emma sat down on a large flat rock, staring out at the Bay and listening to the rhythmic lap of waves on shore. Joel hunkered down and skipped pebbles across the water.

"I brought Brenda here," he said at length.

"I know."

"So how come you didn't say anything?"

"Because you seemed determined to argue with me, and I figured things didn't go too well."

"Yeah, well, you figured right." He skipped another stone across the water. "She started crying again, and then that made Mike cry."

Emma waited, then said, "Just the fact that she came at all is a good sign, isn't it?"

"I bribed her to get her here," he said, sighing. "Her

younger sister Lynn wants to marry a waterman from around here, a guy I know, and her family wants me to talk him out of it." Emma heard the *plop-plop-plop* of another stone. "I told her I'd try if she'd come to see her son. Sure was a big success," he added wryly.

"Well, you got her here," Emma observed. "That counts for something."

"Yeah, and now I've got my boy upstairs in his bedroom with his eyes all red from crying. It was a great thing I did."

"Don't be so hard on yourself," Emma said. "You did the right thing."

"You think so?" he asked after a bit. Before she could answer, he said, "Come here." He stood up and drew her to him, resting his chin on the top of her head. "You smell good," he murmured.

"Well, I don't feel so good," she complained. "I spent the evening with Louis Richter, mostly because I was out of sorts with you."

"Why?" he asked. "Why were you out of sorts with me?"

"Because you surprised me with your jousting tournament and gave me a rose and then you just left me at your party while you took your ex-wife inside." There. She'd aired her grievances, and she waited to see what he'd make of that.

"I see," he said slowly. "Do you think I could make it up to you?"

"I don't see how," she said, but she was teasing him now. Already she felt better, just having him hold her like this.

"Well, let me try anyway," he suggested. He tilted her head up to his, and in the moonlight she could see his gentle smile. "You know," he said softly. "I don't know what I'd do without you." His mouth brushed hers and then something hungry was unleashed inside both of them, and the kiss deepened until Emma thought she would be consumed by the flames that seemed to leap between their bodies. They were both breathless when his mouth finally left hers, and they stared at each other in the night.

"Don't leave me, Emma," he whispered.

"No," she promised. "I won't."

CHAPTER TEN

"*He's* at the door again," Mrs. Grundy announced from the hall outside Emma's bedroom.

"What on earth does he want at this hour?" Emma grumbled sleepily. Sunrise was imminent in the light gray of the sky, but Emma wasn't inclined to get out of bed to check.

"He didn't say," Mrs. Grundy said dryly.

Apparently Joel had followed her upstairs, because his voice came from behind Mrs. Grundy. "Emma, I need your help."

"You can't come up here!" Mrs. Grundy pronounced in outrage, turning on Joel as though he was snapping pictures for the *National Enquirer.* "We aren't dressed!"

"It's all right, Mrs. Grundy," Emma said. "I'll take him downstairs." She pulled on her terry cloth robe and hurried past Mrs. Grundy who was still clutching the lapels of her red-plaid flannel robe in offended modesty. "You love making scenes, don't you?" she whispered to Joel as she led him downstairs.

"Aw, come on, Emma," he said in dejection. "You don't think I enjoyed that, do you?" She gave him a stern look, and he was abashed enough to grin. "Yeah, well, maybe a little," he amended. "You have nice legs, you know that?"

"You're going to get Mrs. Grundy all riled again," Emma warned him, pulling him into the kitchen when she heard Mrs. Grundy's carpet slippers padding downstairs after them. "Now what is going on?"

"Everybody's down with the flu," he said. "The boys and Mrs. Gamble, too. I was wondering if you could come stay with Cory and Mike."

"How sick are they?" Emma asked worriedly. "Should you call a doctor?"

"I already did. The doctor said it's going around and to give them plenty of fluids, some aspirin substitute and whatever they feel like eating." He raked a hand through his hair. "I've got to go out today, Emma. I've got a whole mess of crab pots to do. Can you stay with the boys?"

"Sure," she said without hesitating. "You go on. I'll get dressed and go straight over."

"You're a life saver, you know that?" he asked, grinning again. He pulled her to him and planted a loud kiss on her nose.

"Joel!" she admonished him, knowing he did it just for Mrs. Grundy's benefit.

"I couldn't help it," he swore, still grinning as he whacked her soundly on the bottom and left the kitchen, humming. "Good morning, Mrs. Grundy," he said innocently on his way out.

Mrs. Grundy was still clutching her lapels in disapproval when Emma hurried past her to get dressed.

The boys were supposed to stay in bed and rest, and Emma finally moved them to the same room in single beds after they kept her running between bedrooms, delivering messages to each other. On what must be her twentieth trip upstairs, she took glasses of Kool Aid and a giant puzzle to keep them occupied. On the thirtieth trip she took a portable TV and a bowl of popcorn. Next came a new box of tissues and some cough drops. By afternoon Emma was ready for a nap.

"No requests for at least an hour," she told them. "I'm going to lie down. Call me if you're about to throw up. Otherwise, let me sleep."

She lay down on the couch downstairs and fell asleep thinking about the first time she'd slept on this couch and how aggravated Joel Rivers had been with her. Emma smiled in her sleep. She briefly woke once when she thought she heard the phone ringing, but it stopped, and she drifted back to sleep.

The next thing she knew Joel was kneeling beside the couch, stroking her hair. It was late afternoon by the light coming through the curtains. "What time is it?" Emma asked. "I didn't mean to sleep all day."

"It's all right. I checked on the boys and they're fine." He looked down at the floor and when he looked back at Emma he was smiling crookedly. "There is one slight problem, though."

"What?" Emma sat up, rubbing her eyes with the back of her hand.

"Well, apparently Sunny called while you were sleeping."

"Nothing's wrong, is it?" Emma asked worriedly.

"No, not really." He cleared his throat. "If you don't call her and your Aunt Charlotte coming out here in two days a problem."

"What!?"

Joel smiled wryly. "Cory took the call and I guess he gave her an embellished account of our boat accident and how we were stranded, and then he topped it off by informing her that he and Mike were deathly ill."

Emma groaned. "Oh, Lord. No wonder she's coming out. And she's bringing Aunt Charlotte?"

"That's what Cory said." He rocked back on his heels

and gave her a hopeful look. "Is that bad?"

Emma groaned, and Joel laughed. "I take it that's bad," he said. "Well, come on, honey. Someone's got to help me clean up this house if I'm going to meet your family and not have them think I'm not good enough for their Emma."

He pulled her to her feet, and she couldn't stop looking into those laughing green eyes. He was interested in making an impression on her family, and Emma didn't know what to make of that. But she knew she liked the way his hands held hers and the way he kept looking at her face and grinning.

Aunt Charlotte and Sunny were squabbling when they got out of the battered blue Chevy at Joel's house, and Emma smiled wryly at Joel from their greeting position on the front porch. Sunny reached back into the car to extricate Melinda from her car seat, and still she and Aunt Charlotte fired verbal potshots at each other over whose fault it was anyway that they'd nearly missed finding the ferry to Thorn Haven.

"Well, hello," Emma finally said, hurrying down the steps toward them, and both women turned to enfold her in a three-way embrace, all of them laughing.

"Are you all right?" Aunt Charlotte asked suddenly, leaning back to look at Emma and pat her cheek.

"Oh, yes, fine. I'm glad to see you, but you didn't have to drive all the way out here."

"Well, we would have been here sooner," Sunny said, "but *someone* didn't read the map right. And that little old man on the ferry wouldn't take credit cards."

"I would've read the map right if you hadn't spilled your soda all over it at lunch," Aunt Charlotte complained. "You wiped out a whole highway."

Emma laughed, thinking how Sunny's maps always ended up with food stains on them. "Come here," she said. "I want you to meet Joel."

He was coming down the steps, grinning self-consciously, his new jeans clinging to lean hips and long legs. Emma found herself feeling proud that he looked so good. He had worked hard on the Bay this morning and then came home to shower and wash his hair and dress in the jeans and a blue T-shirt. His hair was still slightly damp, curling onto his forehead, and his eyes were as green as emeralds. He was such a handsome man.

"Oh," said Aunt Charlotte, for once at a loss for words as Joel shook her hand at the introduction.

"Oh," Sunny echoed, and Emma hid her smile. They were impressed.

Cory came running from behind the house, Mike trailing along as fast as he could on his braces. Both had recovered from the flu and were as energetic as ever. Sunny hugged her son, and he proudly introduced Mike to a warm hello from Sunny and Aunt Charlotte. "Come see the ducks!" Cory implored them. "They've got a nest by the water. Come on!"

When Cory had dragged Emma's family away, Joel cleared his throat and looked worried. "So what do you think?" he asked Emma. "Did I do all right?"

She had to laugh. "You did great. They were impressed."

"Really?" He was beginning to smile.

"Yeah, really." She gave him a punch on the shoulder, and then they went to see the ducks, too.

Emma helped Sunny and her aunt unpack in the upstairs guest room after the ducks and the Bay had been duly admired. "So where's your room?" Aunt Charlotte asked bluntly.

Emma felt the blood warming her neck and cheeks. "I stay at a boarding house across the road." She avoided looking at her aunt.

"And why not here?" Aunt Charlotte was apparently interested in this and not about to let it drop.

Emma cleared her throat. "Joel invited me to stay here," she said carefully, "but I thought . . . I mean it might not look right."

"You're in love with him, aren't you?" Aunt Charlotte probed.

Oh, God, Emma thought. *Is it written all over my face?*

"In love?" Sunny cried, rushing to hug her sister. "Good Lord, Em. What happened when you two got marooned?"

"I don't think she wants to talk about it," Aunt Charlotte observed.

"Well, thank you for that much," Emma said, laughing.

"In love?" Sunny repeated. "Oh, Em, that's wonderful."

"No, it isn't," Aunt Charlotte interrupted. "There's a problem, isn't there?"

"Well, I don't know," Emma said, hesitating. Then she decided there was no point in hedging, since Aunt Charlotte would ask Joel if Emma wasn't forthcoming with satisfactory answers. "Joel was married before . . . and his wife couldn't deal with the kind of life he leads. His mother apparently had a rough time of it, too."

"And he thinks you can't cut the mustard," Aunt Charlotte surmised, drawing herself up to her full height of four feet, ten inches. "Well, maybe I ought to have a talk with Joel Rivers."

"No, no, Aunt Charlotte," Emma cried. "Don't do that."

Emma was saved from further protests as Charles the cat meandered into the room and rubbed against Aunt Charlotte's leg, purring. "Well, aren't you the handsome devil?" Aunt Charlotte said, picking him up and stroking him. "Seems like good looks run in the family around here, " she said, looking at Emma significantly.

"The Henley Family Curse," Sunny said suddenly, clutching Emma's arm. "Oh, God, it's the curse again."

"Oh, come on," Emma said weakly.

But Aunt Charlotte was nodding her head. "Sounds like it to me. You love him and he doesn't want to get married. It's the Curse all right."

"What are you going to do?" Sunny said, picking up Melinda who had begun fussing.

Emma sighed. "I just might resign from the Henley family."

Joel had to tend bar that night, so he took everyone with him and insisted that they order the crab feast from the tavern kitchen. Aunt Charlotte and Sunny stared when a plank of freshly boiled crabs in their shell were brought to the table, and Emma hid her smile. Joel was standing by the table, and he exchanged an amused look with Emma. Cory and Mike dug right in, each taking a crab and cracking it under Aunt Charlotte's watchful eyes.

"Do you . . . do you eat this?" Aunt Charlotte asked Emma uncertainly.

"Emma helped me sort crabs on the boat before the storm," Joel said. "Then we boiled some and ate them after the wreck."

"You don't say," Aunt Charlotte said, hanging on his every word.

"Were you stranded long?" Sunny asked delicately.

"Long enough to get to know each other," Joel said, his green eyes ablaze with mischief. "You see, it was pouring rain and we had just this little tarp for shelter—"

"Don't you have to get to work?" Emma prodded him, not missing the way Aunt Charlotte and Sunny gave him their undivided attention.

"Juice is handling things just fine," he informed her, grinning and sitting down at the table between her and Aunt Charlotte. "Emma, why don't you tell your family how to tell a sook from a Jimmy? She's turning into a great culler," he informed the rest of them with a grin.

"Emma swam to the boat and called for help on the CB," Mike added. "They'd been there all night."

Emma groaned mentally. This was not helping at all. Sunny and Aunt Charlotte would be making up rice packets for the wedding next.

"That must have been quite . . . an ordeal," Aunt Charlotte said diplomatically. "Emma will have to tell me all about it sometime—in detail."

Much to Emma's relief, Juice called Joel and he had to go tend bar, and Emma was left to show Aunt Charlotte and Sunny how to eat crab in the shell. Emma pretended not to notice, but Aunt Charlotte kept throwing her sideways glances all during the meal.

Emma took them back to the house after they ate, and they sat on the porch talking about things back in Iowa. The boys were in the small shed behind the house tinkering with an old gocart of Joel's. Charles had taken a liking to Aunt Charlotte and now enjoyed the favored privilege of sitting in her lap.

"How are things at the store?" Emma asked.

"Taking care of themselves," Aunt Charlotte said. "You know, you ought to take that sell offer."

"What did you do, tell everyone?" Emma accused Sunny who shrugged and gave one of her it's-not-really-my-fault smiles. "And what do I do if I sell the store?" Emma said.

"You could marry your young man," Aunt Charlotte said. "I think he's going to come around to that—by and by."

"Well, I'm glad you have my life all figured out," Emma retorted, not at all sure that things would work out that way. She'd learned a long time ago that it wasn't enough just to want something. You didn't always get what you wanted.

It was after midnight when Joel came home from the bar. Emma was sitting on the porch alone, feeling a comfortable sense of belonging here. No doubt Mrs. Grundy would give her a fish-eyed look when she finally went back to her room, but the heck with that. Sunny and Aunt Charlotte had gone to bed, and Melinda was asleep in the same room in Mike's old crib. The boys had gone upstairs hours ago, whispering conspiratorially. After a few thumps from their room things had quieted down.

"Hey there," Joel said softly, smiling and stretching on the bottom step. He looked so tired, and Emma stood up, already feeling a hunger fill her heart just from looking at him.

"You want something to eat?" she asked softly, her eyes on his beautiful face.

"No." He shook his head. Slowly he came up the steps, and Emma's heart pounded against her ribs. His eyes never strayed from her own, and she read such wonderful promises hidden deep in those green depths. *Love me, love me, love me,* her heart beat in a heavy, intoxicated cadence.

He paused a moment at the top step, and his mouth crooked up at one side. "Lord, but you're nice to come home to, you know that?" Before she could answer he put his arms around her and drew her close. Emma's eyes closed as she rested her head against his chest. He smelled of the wind and the Bay and the faint odor of cigarette smoke in the bar. Her fingers curled around his shirt, and she pressed her face tightly against him. She wanted to stand like this forever. Joel's hand was stroking her hair, and he sighed, a deep rumble in his chest.

"You feel so right just like this," he whispered, nuzzling his chin against her hair.

"I know," she murmured. "It's like I've been looking for something for so long, and I'm so tired, and then all of a sudden I've found it."

She was going to say more, to tell him she loved him and the life he led was what she wanted, but she didn't get the chance. Footsteps pounded across the yard, the air broken by hard breathing. Cory came to an agitated halt at the foot of the steps. His hair was disheveled, his eyes wide and anxiety-ridden. Emma stepped away from Joel, worried. "Cory, you're shaking like a leaf. What's wrong?"

He looked from one to the other as if afraid to speak. "It's—it's Mike," he said haltingly, his lips quivering. "We were working—that old gocart—fixing it up—and tonight Mike wanted—to try it out." He stopped and swallowed hard, his breath still coming in hard gasps. "It's all my fault—I should have—stopped him." He was beginning to cry now.

"It's all right, Cory," Joel said in a quiet voice, and Emma glanced at him. His eyes were riveted on Cory, and his anxiety was palpable. "What happened?"

"We snuck out the back door tonight," he said miserably, the tears rolling down his face. "We—I pushed the gocart—down to the field. Mike wanted—to ride it. And I let him. He ran over a rock—and the gocart overturned." The words came tumbling out now. "He's pinned underneath and I can't get him out." He broke into sobs, and Emma exchanged an anxious look with Joel.

"Take care of Cory," Joel said quickly. "I'm taking the truck."

"Don't leave me here!" Cory begged. "Please!"

Joel hesitated a second, and his eyes met Emma's again. "Let us go with you," she said quietly.

He nodded. "Come on."

It felt like it took forever for the truck to bump over the field. Cory was snuffling quietly between Joel and Emma, and Emma absently put her arm around him and rubbed his shoulder. *Mike has to be all right,* she told herself over and over. It would kill Joel if anything happened to him. A long time ago Emma's father had told her that one can't make bargains with God, but Emma found herself trying anyway. *Let Mike be okay,* she prayed silently and fervently, *and I'll give up Joel if I have to. Just don't take Mike from Joel.*

The headlights swung across a wooden fence as the truck turned, and for an instant the metal of the gocart glittered in the light. It was upside down on top of Mike, the wheels eerily still in the air. Joel brought the truck to a halt, and they all jumped out. "Mike!" Cory called. "Mike! We're here!"

Joel was kneeling by the gocart. "It's all right, son. We're here. You're going to be okay." Emma felt tears gather in her eyes as Joel pressed a hand to Mike's hair, a gentle, tender gesture of a father. "Dad," Mike said softly. "I knew you'd come. I'm sorry . . . I know I shouldn't have . . ."

"Don't talk now," Joel said. "Later." He tested an edge of the gocart, hefting it slightly to get the feel. "Okay," he said. "You ready, tiger?"

"Yeah," Mike said quietly. "Anytime, Dad."

Emma put her hands over Cory's shoulders and held

him against her as they both watched Joel. She could feel Cory shaking slightly, and she absently rubbed his shoulder in sympathy.

Joel strained to lift the gocart, and Emma couldn't breathe as she watched his muscles strain against his shirt. His legs were braced apart, his whole body in an attitude of raw power and determination. He got one side of the gocart into the air and braced his shoulder against it, pushing until it was resting on two wheels, clear of Mike. Then he pushed the gocart so it landed on all four wheels away from Mike. The next instant he was kneeling by his son. "How're you doing?"

"Okay, Dad." Mike managed a weak smile.

"I'm going to get a board from the back of the truck," Joel said. "I'll be right back. Just hang on."

Emma held Mike's hand while Joel was gone, noting that the boy's eyes followed his father all the way to the truck. Emma glanced off to the right and saw the shadowy figure of Cory picking up Mike's metal crutches from near the fence. His shoulders were slumped, his head down, and Emma knew how awful he must feel right now. "Cory," she called softly. "Why don't you come over and stay with Mike?"

But he shook his head without turning around. "I'll wait in the truck," he said, his voice dejected.

Joel was back with the board, and Emma helped him slide it beneath Mike before they lifted him. Cory was already sitting in the front of the truck when they carried Mike to the back. "I'll ride back here and hold him steady," Joel said. He squeezed Emma's hand and looked into her eyes. "Can you drive the truck?"

She nodded. "Yes. Don't worry," she added softly.

He squeezed her hand again. "Go back to the main road

and take a right. The doctor's office is about a mile down the road. I'll knock on the window when we get close." He took a deep breath, his eyes locking with hers. "Drive slowly, especially on the bridge over Quail Creek. There are some potholes there."

She absorbed his instructions automatically, still looking into his face and saying her silent prayer that Mike would be all right. "Okay," she said. "Let's go."

She drove intently, scanning the road anxiously for any bump or pothole that would jar the truck. Cory sat in abject silence, staring out the side window, and Emma didn't know what to say to him. His reflection in the glass was pinched and white, and his hands were clenched on his lap.

Joel tapped on the window, and Emma slowed the truck even more, seeing the white sign ahead in the yard. She turned in and took a deep breath. *Please let Mike be all right.*

When Sunny and Aunt Charlotte came downstairs the next morning Joel and Emma were sitting at the kitchen table holding hands, their fingers laced together next to cups of cold coffee.

"My God!" Sunny said, setting Melinda down on the floor. "You two look exhausted. Were you up all night?"

Aunt Charlotte cleared her throat pointedly, but Sunny ignored her.

"There was an accident," Emma said wearily. Seeing the look of alarm on their faces, she quickly added, "Cory's all right. And Mike is going to be okay, too."

"What happened?" Sunny asked, sitting down at the table while Aunt Charlotte poured coffee.

"Mike and Cory have been tinkering around with an old gocart I had in the shed," Joel said. "They snuck out late last night and took it down to the field. Mike talked Cory into helping him ride it and he crashed."

"My word," Aunt Charlotte said. "Is he hurt?"

Joel shook his head. "The doctor admitted him to the hospital for observation, but he thinks he can come home today."

"Well, thank God for that," Aunt Charlotte said. "Where's Cory? I'd like to give that boy a good talking to for pulling a stunt like that with Mike."

"He feels bad enough," Emma said. "He went to bed as soon as we got home from the hospital." She gave Sunny a meaningful look. "Maybe you ought to go up and talk to him. You know, let him know he's not so bad."

"All right," Sunny said dubiously.

When she'd gone upstairs Aunt Charlotte fixed Emma with a penetrating look. "What's got into that boy anyway? Sunny was telling me he got himself into trouble out here."

"He's had a hard time," Emma said evasively.

"He's a good boy," Joel added. "He'll be all right."

Sunny's footsteps clattered down the stairs and she stopped in the doorway, a baffled expression on her face. "He's not there," she said, looking from Emma to Joel.

Joel sat up quickly and glanced at Emma. "Not there?" he said.

"His bed doesn't look like it's been slept in," Sunny said.

"Where could he be?" Emma said, her fingers tightening on Joel's.

"I think I know," he said. "Mike told me he and Cory like to go out to the old pier, especially Cory." He let go of Emma's hand and stood up, frowning as he ran a hand through his hair. "He's really upset over the accident. I'd better go talk to him."

Emma put her hand on his arm. "Wait." She looked at

Sunny who was staring at her anxiously. "Why don't Sunny and I go? We have . . . things to talk about with Cory."

Joel nodded. "Yeah. I think that's good."

Sunny went to get a scarf for her hair, and Joel walked Emma out on the porch. He stopped and turned her to face him, his hands on her arms. "Emma, I meant it about being glad you were with me last night."

"I know," she said, laying her head against his chest. "It's so hard, isn't it? Wanting your son to be independent and not wanting him to get hurt." She looked up at him, her heart clenching at the shadows in his eyes.

"It's damn tough," he said, and she heard all the frustration in his voice. "I want him to find his own limits instead of setting them for him and it tears me up inside watching him try to do things other kids take for granted."

"He's a gutsy kid," Emma said.

"Don't feel sorry for him," Joel said, looking down at her.

"No. Not for him or his father."

He brushed her hair back and ran his lips over her forehead. "What's a waterman doing with an Iowa minister's daughter?" he teased her, and she smiled.

They heard Sunny opening the screen door and reluctantly pulled apart. "Are you sure he's all right?" Sunny asked hesitantly.

"He's fine," Emma said. "But he wants to talk to you."

Emma knew where the old pier was, and she led Sunny there along the shore of the Bay, thinking each step of the way about the waterman who was so dear to her.

The pier was surrounded by cattails, and Joel never used it anymore. Emma looked around, her feet sinking in the soft earth, and thought how familiar and comfortable all of this was to her now. She was so afraid of the water when she first came here, and now that fear was gone, gone with the sense of emptiness that had dogged her so long. Joel and this place were everything she needed.

Cory must have been sitting on the other side of the pier because he stood up as they approached with rustling movements through the cattails. His jeans and sneakers were caked with mud, and matted grass clung to his face and hair. "I guess you're pretty mad, huh?" he said, jamming his hands in his pockets and looking at them anxiously.

"Oh, Cory, of course not," Sunny said, hurrying to enfold him in her arms. "How could you think that?" She knelt beside him and brushed his hair from his forehead.

" 'Cause of what happened with Mike," he said, staring down at the ground. "It was my fault for letting him on the gocart. And for what I did . . . before you came. With the stores." This last was obviously hard for him to say, and Sunny tipped his chin up to her. "I . . . stole some things," he got out.

"Why, honey?" she asked softly.

He shrugged, his thin shoulders sagging as with the weight of the world. "I don't know. I didn't really want the stuff. And I felt worse after I took it."

"Were you lonely?" Sunny asked.

Cory nodded. "Yeah. That, too."

"What else?" Sunny prompted softly.

He toed the ground and frowned. "Like no one wanted me," he said in a small voice. "And bad 'cause Dad left."

Sunny hugged him to her. "Listen to me, fella," she said in fierce emotion. "It's not your fault your dad left, and you'll always be his son and he'll love you no matter where you are or what you do." She held him away from her and lowered her head to look into his face. "And *I* love you more than you'll ever know. If anyone should feel guilty it's me for getting so busy with Melinda that I didn't have time for you. You'll always be my first baby, Cory, and that's a special thing to be. You're my son, and I'm proud of you."

Emma stood back from them, but she could hear what Sunny said, and she could see the abashed but happy smile that Cory tried to tame.

"And don't feel bad about Mike's accident," Sunny said. "If you two hadn't tried to ride that gocart you wouldn't be normal ten-year-old boys."

"Is Joel pretty ticked off at me?" Cory asked, worry creeping into his voice again.

"No, honey. He understands. He was worried about Mike, but everything's okay now. Mike's coming home today."

"Yeah?" A full smile burgeoned on Cory's face. "Can I go when they pick him up?"

"I'm pretty sure you can," Sunny said, laughing and hugging Cory again. "Come on. Let's go back to the house and get you cleaned up."

"I don't have to take a bath, do I?" he complained, his happiness dissolving in the wake of this new development.

"You don't want to stink up the hospital, do you?" Sunny asked. "They might not let you inside."

"I could wait in the truck," he said hopefully.

"No deal," Sunny told him, ruffling his hair as she led him back toward Emma. Sunny's eyes met her sister's over Cory's head, and Emma nodded and smiled.

They walked back to the house, and Cory ran ahead. "They can resolve things fast when they're young, can't they?" Emma said, her eyes automatically looking for Joel outside.

"Emma, stop thinking like that," Sunny said sternly, turning to face her sister.

"Like what?"

"Like it's over between you and Joel. I can hear it in your voice. And any fool who saw him hanging onto your hand like a lifeline this morning knows he's going to beg you to marry him."

Emma shook her head even as she smiled. "I don't know. I've had this odd feeling . . . ever since the accident last night." She didn't say anymore, and Sunny didn't press her.

CHAPTER ELEVEN

Emma was restless the Sunday that Sunny, Melinda, and Aunt Charlotte left for the drive back to Iowa. Cory was staying to finish the football camp, and Emma was staying, too. Sunny had hugged her when they left and whispered in her ear, "I'm glad someone's finally beating that Henley Family Curse."

The boys announced that they were invited to a pizza party at a friend's house—Mike had been given the official okay by his doctor—and Joel dropped them off. He came in the back door whistling when he got back, and Emma looked up from the cake she was decorating. Tomorrow was Mrs. Gamble's birthday, and the boys wanted to surprise her when she arrived.

Joel was grinning, and Emma couldn't help smiling. "What?" she said, piping the last of the scallop border on with icing.

"We're alone," he said, grinning broader and raising his eyebrows.

"So we are." She walked over to him solemnly and couldn't resist touching his nose with her icing-covered finger. She laughed when he tried to see the end of his nose.

"Mmmm," he said, wiping it off and sticking his finger in his mouth. "Did anybody ever tell you you can cook?"

"It's been mentioned before by a certain waterman and his son," she said, licking her own finger. Her cooking efforts so far had been greeted with wild enthusiasm, much to her delight.

"You have some icing there," he said, nodding toward her mouth.

Emma licked her lips and couldn't find it. "Where?"

"There," he said softly, his smile beguiling. He lowered his head to hers and nibbled on her lips. His mouth roved over hers, tasting and tantalizing, and finally he raised his head. "More icing," he explained with straight-faced guile.

"I'll be glad to spread a little more on," she murmured breathlessly.

"Hey," he said softly, his hands slipping down to cup her bottom. "Let's go out by the water, okay?"

She was more interested in having him remove icing from her lips at the moment, but she nodded and he grabbed her hand and pulled her out the door. "Look!" she called excitedly, dragging him to a halt and pointing to the sky. An osprey circled over the Bay behind the house, and suddenly it dived with a flash of talons, striking the surface of the water and rising again. "I saw an osprey the first day I was here," she said, feeling that same sense of freedom and exhilaration.

"Come on, lady," he called, pulling her after him. "You can admire the ospreys later."

They were both laughing as they raced to the water, and Emma kicked off her sandals. She was wearing white cotton slacks, and she pulled up the legs as they ran along the shore. Joel stopped and turned to her. The laughter died when she saw the expression in his eyes, and her heart pounded in her throat. *She loved this man so much.* She laced her hands behind his neck and indulged in the luxury of just looking at him. They had taken Emma's family out for breakfast, and Joel still wore brown chinos and a long-sleeved light-green shirt that he'd rolled up to his elbows. His jaw was clean and smooth from shaving that morning, and his black hair fell forward onto his forehead. And those eyes. Those beautiful, gentle green eyes watching her. Lord, did he know how much she loved him?

He might have heard her thoughts the way his eyes darkened and fastened on her mouth. His hands touched her waist and drew her toward him. "Emma," he said so softly and hesitantly that she hardly heard him. And then he was kissing her, his mouth traveling over hers in urgency, his breath hypnotically mingling with her own. His hands trembled at her waist, and Emma felt his desire against her legs, her own need for him rising in aching swiftness. He brought forth something in her that she'd never known she possessed, some primitive passion that shook her as fiercely as the storm they'd weathered on the island. His touch was all flame, leaving her knees weak and her body craving more of that fire he ignited in her.

He was pushing up her peach cotton sweater. The sun shone on his bronze skin, so dark against the creaminess of her own flesh under the sweater, and his thumbs flicked gently over the thin lace of her bra, bringing her nipples to hardness. She groaned and ran her hands over the hard ridges of his back muscles.

They slid down to the ground on their knees in one accord, and he kissed her again, demanding and tender at the same time, his tongue entering her mouth to tempt her own to touch and mate in return. His teeth caught her lower lip and gently nibbled, making her moan. With a lover's knowledge he instinctively knew the sweet places so receptive to his touch.

Joel lay on his side and pulled her down with him, running his hands through her hair and kissing her throat as she arched her head back. "Emma. I want you," he told her fiercely, his voice as possessive as his touch. "Do you know how much I need you, honey?"

Yes, yes. She was consumed by the same flames, a fire of desire so strong that she would give him everything she was, anything he wanted of her.

"I . . . love you, Joel," she whispered, because she could tell him nothing less than the truth. "I love you so much."

"God help me, I love you, too," he breathed hoarsely. "I can't help it, Emma. I might as well stop breathing as stop trying not to love you. I don't want to hurt you . . ."

"You won't," she told him, shaking her head. "Don't think about that." She told herself that he knew her, that he knew she could live his life, that everything would be all right. And she ignored that nagging voice inside her that warned that sometimes even love wasn't enough.

Their breathing was shaky, their fingers trembling, as they touched each other and then pressed their palms together as they kissed. The flames inside them burned more fiercely, and Joel slid up her sweater, pulling it over her head. He unhooked her bra and peeled it off. The grass and earth were soft and yielding beneath Emma's back, and the breeze touched her bare skin ever so gently, fueling her already heated blood.

His mouth closed on one swelling breast, circling it with his tongue and sucking as her fingers dug into his shoulders. "Love me," she whispered, her breath harsh and unfamiliar to her ears. "I want you inside me." She was hungry to hold him, to take him deep within her, and to give him herself.

He undid her pants and pulled them off, then her underpants, his hands stroking her legs. The tension of wanting him was unbearable, and Emma tried to unbutton his shirt. Her fingers didn't seem capable of such a simple action and she ended up pulling open the last two buttons, her hands sliding to his bare chest and pressing against the dark hair. He stood up to remove his pants, his eyes never leaving her.

His body was so strong and male, and she loved every inch of it. His was a life of work, and it showed in each taut muscle and sinew.

He came to her then, kneeling down to kiss her thighs as his hands held her hips still. Emma's fingers tangled in his hair and then feathered shakily down his shoulders and chest.

"Emma," he said, his eyes a smoky green, hazy with desire. "I want to give you so much . . . I want everything for you."

"You're enough. You're all I want. Don't you know that?" She managed a smile through her burgeoning passion, and she drew him to her. He was poised over her an instant, blocking out the sun, and then he was inside her, bringing the sun with him. He and his lovemaking became her world.

Their rhythm on the ground became the rhythm of the water in the Chesapeake and the rhythm of the seasons. It was timeless and unstoppable and it carried them to the sky itself and then beyond.

When the crest of pleasure took them Emma trembled and clung to Joel as though afraid he would somehow slip away. He breathed her name reverently against her throat as he kissed her and smoothed her hair from her face. "I love you," he cried hoarsely. "My Emma."

They lay languidly in the sun, not caring about the grass or earth that clung to their skin. The water lapped softly near them, and a gull cried as it flew out over the water. Emma's eyes roved possessively over her lover and then her hands followed as he laughed and told her she had an insatiable appetite. What she had, she told herself, was love.

★ ★ ★ ★ ★

When Joel went to pick up the boys, Emma called Sunny. She smiled contentedly as she listened to the soft *whooshing* on the line as circuits worked to connect her with Iowa. She made up her mind today—she would sell the store. It was time to be done with the past.

"Hello?"

It was an unfamiliar, young female voice, and Emma said, "Is this Sunny's house?"

"Oh, yeah, sure. I'm the babysitter. Sunny went on a fishing trip today."

Emma grinned as she imagined Sunny fishing. No doubt she'd have five husky young men vying to clean her fish by the end of the day. "This is her sister Emma. Would you have her call me when she gets back? She knows the number."

"Yeah, sure. Say, since you're her sister—do you know where she keeps the potato chips?"

"Far right cabinet. Top shelf."

"Oh, great! Thanks."

Emma was humming to herself after she hung up and began cleaning up the bowls used in her cake baking. She felt really good for the first time in ages, free and happy like the osprey that had served as an omen for her trip. She had come home to something she'd never had in her life, and it felt so good.

"Hey, wow, cake!" Cory enthused as he burst through the door first. "Can we have a piece?"

"No, you can't," Emma said, feigning sternness. "It's for Mrs. Gamble's birthday tomorrow. Remember, you wanted to surprise her?"

"I think she'd still be surprised if we ate just one piece," Cory tried.

Emma laughed. "Lucky for you I made some cupcakes with the extra batter." She doled out the cupcakes as her men lined up. Cory, Mike, and Joel. She laughed when Joel kissed her on the cheek and said, "Thank you, ma'am." He took a big bite of the cupcake, rolled his eyes in ecstasy, then said, "Boys, now what can we do for Emma to show our appreciation so she'll make us cupcakes again?"

"You could do the dishes," Emma suggested.

"Naw," Joel said. "That wasn't what I had in mind."

"I know!" Cory said. "We could take her out for ice cream to go with the cake."

Joel shook his head. "I had something different in mind." Emma saw the twinkle in his eyes and wondered what he was up to now. This was her Joel, always springing surprises on her.

"Let's take her to the movies, Dad," Mike suggested, and Emma smiled.

"No," Joel said slowly, building the suspense. "I thought maybe we ought to show her turkling."

"Yeah!" Cory cried. "That's a great idea!"

"Come on!" Mike called, already pivoting on his crutches.

"Dare I ask?" Emma said, giving Joel her best *Now what is this all about?* look. "Turkling? This isn't something that requires a snorkel and mask, is it?"

He laughed and looped an arm around her shoulders. "Come on, Kendrick. You'll find out."

Whatever turkling was, it apparently didn't involve any special equipment. Joel led her and the boys down to the water, nudging her and winking when they passed the place where they'd made love such a short time ago. She felt the heat rising in her, and she grinned at him.

"All right now," he said, mischief in his voice, his face

solemn but on the verge of a quirking smile, "I need some quiet."

They were standing on a marshy section with reeds and cattails where the water oozed among the grasses. Joel kicked off his shoes and rolled up his pants. Then he waded out into the water, his legs flexed and apart, and stood surveying his surroundings, hands on hips. Emma knew he was showing off for her, and she loved it.

He gave them one last teasing look over his shoulder, and then he cupped his hands around his mouth and began yelling at the top of his voice, "Yo! Yo! Yo!" He started clapping his hands together loudly, still hollering at the top of his lungs, and Emma wondered what on earth was the purpose of this ear-splitting display. Was he trying to scare every fish in the Bay into the next state?

Suddenly a small head appeared at the surface of the water, and the boys started shouting too. Joel lunged toward the whatever-it-was and in a split second snatched it from the water. Emma stared in amazement as he turned around, carefully holding an irritated snapping turtle well away from him. He came toward Emma, holding out the turtle and grinning, and she backed away. "Get that thing away from me!" she said, and the boys dissolved in helpless laughter.

"It's just a turkle, Aunt Emma," Cory teased her mirthfully, and Emma grimaced.

"It looks more like a very angry, ferocious turtle," she said. Feet and head waving, the turtle seemed intent on biting anything it could reach.

Grinning, he put the turtle back in the water and let it go. "If you liked it, I could catch another one for a pet for you," he suggested, turning around and walking toward her, trying oh-so-hard not to laugh.

"You can just stuff that smirk back in your mouth, Rivers," she advised him. "Because I can tell you I am not impressed."

"Not one little bit?" he asked, his smile escaping again as he stopped in front of her, the bottom of his pants wet where he'd rolled them up to his knees.

"Well . . . maybe a little," she hedged, looking down at the ground because she was afraid that if she looked into his eyes she would start laughing.

"Dad's a great turkler," Mike said proudly.

"He certainly is," Emma agreed. "He caught a monster turtle."

"Turkle! Not turtle!" Her two youthful critics were chorusing their corrections.

"You can't be a proper Eastern Shore resident unless you say turkle," Joel informed her.

"All right," Emma said. "Turkle. And, by the way, I loved your technique. It was very subtle."

Joel's grin got away from him again. "That's how you get the attention of a snapper. They come up to the surface to see what all the fuss is about and you grab 'em. *Very* carefully. You have to be sure you know which way the spines are facing, so you pick them up from the back."

"Hey, remember that turkle Granddad caught that time in the Mississippi?" Cory said. "Aunt Charlotte made soup out of it."

Emma shook her head. "No, I don't remember that."

Cory frowned a moment, then said, "Oh, yeah. That was when you were in the hospital with that lady."

"She was a psychologist," Emma said automatically, her voice surprisingly level given the turmoil inside her. She was looking at Cory, but every fiber of her being was straining toward Joel. She didn't dare look at him yet, terrified of what she might see in his face. The hospital. Such an innocent word, but she knew what it meant to Joel—it was a sign of weakness, a sign that she would eventually crumble as his mother and Brenda had. And she realized why she had never told him about the hospital—she knew how he would react. She had tried to buy herself enough time for him to know her before she told him, and now her time had run out.

The boys had rapidly lost interest in the conversation and were idly poking around the ground, and Emma finally dared a glance at Joel. He looked away, and her heart constricted. She had seen the hurt in his eyes.

"Why don't we head back to the house and get ready for dinner?" he said, still not looking at Emma. "Do you think you boys could handle hamburgers tonight after pizza for lunch?"

His voice was lifeless, and Emma felt a suffocating despair seep through her, a leaden misery worse than the grief she'd felt after Paul's death. Joel was shutting her out.

The boys were carrying on an exuberant conversation all the way back to the house, alleviating the necessity of Joel and Emma having to talk. He walked apart from her, his shoulders sagging wearily. Emma ached for him to touch her, even to look at her, but she might as well have been back in Iowa.

She touched his sleeve as they mounted the steps, and he finally turned to face her. His eyes were filled with emptiness as he jammed his hands in his rear pockets. They both stood silently until the screen door banged behind the boys.

"Emma," he said, his voice threaded with regret. "I didn't know."

"Listen to me," she said fiercely. "Don't shut me out like this. Let me tell you how it was."

"You don't have to do that," he said quietly, and she could have cried at the polite distance in his voice.

"Yes, I do! I love you! Doesn't that mean anything?" He didn't say anything, and she drew a deep breath. "It was after Paul died," she said, "I was numb, and I just kept working harder and harder to keep the store going. I was lucky—I'd been doing the book work before, so I was used to that. But there were so many other things—things I knew nothing about." She searched his face but could fathom nothing of what he was thinking. "I didn't give myself any free time, any little minute in the day where I might think about Paul or how things were now. I just worked from morning until night, until I was so tired that I fell into bed. Do you know that I used to wake up with my muscles aching from not moving all night? I was that exhausted. And then one day—I started crying. And I couldn't stop. I was in the store, and I finally had to call Sunny to come take over. I went home and lay down on my bed, and I cried all that day. Dad came when Sunny told him, and he took me to the hospital. It wasn't until I met my psychologist, Dr. Morgan, that I began to recover."

"Emma . . . don't . . ."

"Yes," she whispered harshly. "Yes, I have to tell you this. I learned to grieve, and I learned to be strong by not denying my emotions. I'm not the same person who went into that hospital. I'm stronger, Joel, a hell of a lot stronger. And if you don't believe that—then I might as well go back to Iowa right now because you'll always treat me like some fragile piece of china that's going to break." *Oh, God.* She'd said the thing she'd dreaded most. She'd said that it might be over between them. She hadn't realized how hard her heart was pounding until she paused and took a deep, shaky breath.

"Emma," he began and then shook his head, looking off toward the road. "Don't you see? This is killing me, hearing you tell me this. I can't stand to see you hurt. I can't stand to think of you crying—ever."

She stared at him a long moment, hearing the phone ringing inside the house and not really recognizing what it was. There was only this moment and the breaking of her heart. "Joel," she said softly, "are you telling me it's time I went home?"

"I don't—" he began, swinging tortured eyes to her, but his voice broke, and he turned away from her to stride up the steps.

"Hey, Emma," Cory called from the door. "Sunny's on the phone."

Joel wasn't in the living room when Emma gathered herself together and went inside. "Yes?" she said lifelessly into the phone.

"Hey, Em, it's me. What's wrong?"

"Nothing, Sunny."

"Why'd you call? And you sound awful. What's going on?"

"I'm coming home," Emma said wearily.

"Emma Kendrick, you tell me what's happened!"

"I don't want to talk now, Sunny. Really. I'm leaving in the morning."

She hung up and went back outside, not remembering how she got in her car and drove back to Mrs. Grundy's. She packed her suitcase and then lay down on her side of the bed. After a minute the tears began, and she let them flow, slowly and inexorably, down her cheeks and onto the spread.

CHAPTER TWELVE

Joel's face swam before her as she drove through Pennsylvania, and she had to stop once at a Howard Johnson's on the turnpike to wipe away the tears coursing down her face.

Emma had gone to his house the next morning to tell Cory she was leaving. She had thought Joel would be out on the water, but Cory told her he was sitting on the grass behind the house. "My mom called last night," Mike told her, his eyes serious, "and she said my aunt ran away and married that guy. I think everyone's hacked off at my dad." He looked at Cory a moment, then turned to Emma and took a deep breath. "I heard Dad asking her to come see me, and I . . . I guess she wouldn't."

"I'm sorry, Mike," Emma said, hugging him, then turning to Cory and drawing him close. She shut her eyes to squeeze out the images of Joel coping with everything and forced herself to ruffle Cory's hair. "You two take care," she said.

"You'll be back soon, won't you?" Mike asked anxiously, and Emma hesitated.

The boy had been deserted once before—she didn't want to hurt him. But she didn't want to lie either. "I'll try," she said. "I really will."

Mrs. Gamble's cake was still on the counter, and Emma couldn't help smiling slightly as she saw that someone had artfully used a knife to chisel out a small piece from the back.

She went out the door, intending to go straight to her

187

car, but she couldn't stop herself from walking around the side of the house and partway to the water. She stopped by the cherry tree and just looked. Joel was kneeling by the water, his head down, slowly and methodically skipping stones across the flat, blue surface. She wanted so badly to go to him and hold him, but she couldn't. He couldn't share his life with her, and Emma had to go home.

She took a step backward, and as if he'd sensed her presence he turned around. The sun glinted on his black hair, and she could see all the pain etched on his face. *Oh, Joel. It doesn't have to be like this.* He stood up—only some twenty feet away—and Emma felt tears choking her throat. He looked so sad and lonely. He just stood there looking at her, as though memorizing her face, and when the tears blurred Emma's vision so that he was a wavering shadow she turned and hurried back to the car.

She saw an osprey when she crossed the Chesapeake Bay Bridge, but this time she'd lost that feeling of freedom. This time she had lost love.

Now she was home in Iowa, but she felt like those people who are declared clinically dead and then revive. Nothing felt right. Even her skin didn't seem to be her own anymore. The Iowa wind felt too strong and hot, not like the breeze from the Chesapeake. And her eyes seemed to tear up at the slightest provocation. She wondered if she was developing an allergy to corn and wheat.

She threw herself into work at the store with a vengeance. She opened the store at seven in the morning and closed it at ten each night. Then she went into the back room and pored over the bookkeeping records for another two hours.

Football camp ended in late August, and Cory came home on a plane, the biggest adventure of his life, he said.

Emma had promised herself she wouldn't ask about Joel, but the words came out the instant she hugged Cory in the airport. "How are Joel and Mike?"

"Mike's great," Cory said. "We're going to write to each other."

He didn't say anything else, and Sunny's eyes met Emma's over Cory's head. "So how's Mike's dad?" Sunny prompted.

Cory shrugged. "He doesn't talk much anymore. Mike says he's moody. He'd go out and sit by the water every night after Mike and I were in bed. We'd see him when the moon was out, and he'd just sit there. Sometimes he'd throw stones in the water." Cory switched subjects and began giving them an enthusiastic report on the picnic held at the end of football camp and how the kids had pushed Louis Richter into the water. Emma only half heard. Her thoughts were on the man sitting by himself at the water's edge. In her own way she was just as alone and just as miserable.

Sunny came to the store as Emma was closing up one night in October. "Em," she said, leaning against the counter and crossing her arms, "you're driving yourself into the ground working like this. Why don't you sell the store?"

Emma shook her head, barely looking up from the cash register where she was bagging the currency. "And do what then? Sit around until I'm old?"

"Honestly, Em. You could find something else. Something that doesn't drive you all the time. Look at you. You're half dead on your feet. And now that the fuel assistance program started up for the winter you're busier than ever. And what for?"

"So I don't have time to think," Emma said wearily. "I

don't want any time on my hands, Sunny."

"Em, Dad's worried about you."

This was a serious threat, because when the Reverend Henley was worried about something or someone he usually took action. Emma's hands stilled on the register. "Talk to him, Sunny. Tell him I'm okay, will you?"

Sunny sighed. "Em, you love the guy, don't you?"

"Dad? Sure."

"You know who I mean, and you can stop pretending to count money. You've been unfolding and folding that dollar bill so long that George Washington has a permanent frown."

Emma stared down at her hands. "I love him, Sunny. And I don't think I'll ever see him again." She could feel the tears welling up again. "And I don't know how I'm going to live with that."

"Oh, honey, I'm so sorry." Sunny came around the counter and hugged Emma. "Why don't you call him?"

Emma shook her head. "I can't. He has to be the one to decide we'll be together."

"God, you drive a hard bargain, kid," Sunny said in a mournful voice. "Now, if you'd been the ancestor to spill your tankard on that gypsy you probably would have put a curse on her instead of the other way around."

Emma smiled for the first time in weeks.

It had to be the flu. Emma ached from head to toe and every muscle in between. She had felt tired last night after she closed the store and worked on the books, and three of her clients in the fuel assistance program had come into the office with the flu last week. What day was this anyway, Tuesday?

Groaning, she made her way to the bathroom and found

the thermometer, then groped her way back to bed. Her head was spinning from the effort.

She dialed Sunny with the thermometer in her mouth and waited twelve rings for Sunny to answer. "I can't go to the store today," she said sluggishly around the thermometer. "Can you ask Aunt Charlotte to get one of her friends to fill in for me?"

"Is that you, Em?" Sunny said in a groggy voice. "Heavens, what time is it? Oh, good Lord, it's only six a.m."

Emma coughed and the thermometer fell out onto the pillow. Grumbling, she groped until she found it and then held it up to the light from the bedside lamp. "One hundred and two, Sunny," she groaned. "You've got to find someone for me."

"Okay, okay. Give me a few minutes to get some coffee to my brain and I'll take care of it. I'll be over later to check on you."

Emma aimed the receiver in the general direction of the cradle and dropped it. She felt miserable all over. Her head was so heavy she couldn't lift it from the pillow. She must have fallen asleep because the next thing she knew Sunny was beside the bed, clucking in dismay and retrieving the receiver from the floor. She gave Emma some aspirin and a glass of water and mopped her brow with a damp washcloth. Emma feebly smiled her thanks and drifted off to sleep again.

In sleep her feverish limbs clung to Joel on the sunny deck of his boat, and the moisture on her face was the water's spray. He was making love to her, and she felt the first stirrings of joy she'd felt since she'd left Thorn Haven. He was with her, and she clasped him tightly in her arms, willing him never to go away.

Someone was gently sponging her brow again, and she opened her eyes partway, unable to focus at first. "Go on home, Sunny," she said hoarsely. "I'll be okay. What day is it anyway?"

"Wednesday," a deep voice said. "Go back to sleep."

"Joel?" she said through dry lips. She struggled to open her eyes all the way. "Joel!" He was sitting there on the side of her bed in jeans and a black sweater and he looked so tired. "You look awful," she said, frowning. "What are you doing here?"

He smiled crookedly, and some of the weariness left his face. "Your dad called me yesterday. He seemed to think you and I weren't doing too well apart."

"Oh, Lord, I must look terrible." She struggled to get up.

"Lie down," he insisted, taking her shoulders and pushing her gently back. "You need to rest."

"What are you doing here?" she asked, and then she was afraid to hear the answer. Maybe he hadn't come for her after all. Maybe he'd only brought Mike to visit Cory. She looked down at the quilt and his hand holding hers. "Joel— are we—I mean, are you here because of me?" She didn't dare look at him.

"Would you mind if I were?" he asked tentatively.

"Mind?" Her eyes flew to his face, seeing the hesitation and worry there.

"When you left, I wasn't sure you'd want to see me again."

The shadows were there in his face and the sadness and loneliness of a solitary man. Emma squeezed his hand. "I couldn't stay . . . not when I couldn't be part of your life."

"It's not easy, Emma," he said, looking at their hands and then back to her face. "I tried very hard to tell myself that was best for you. But the fact was that I was just plain scared. I was afraid of losing you. I couldn't stand the thought of you leaving me . . . and I was sure you would in time."

"And now?" she asked anxiously. *I need you so much,* her heart cried.

"You're strong, Emma Kendrick, and inside I knew that from the day you swam out to the boat when we were stranded. I don't have a lot to offer you, but you know that." He put aside the washcloth and clasped her hand in both of his. "But what I have is yours, Emma . . . if you want."

"Yes," she said, her heart racing from more than the flu. "I love you so much."

"Tell me again," he said, green eyes shining, a crooked smile touching his mouth. "I can't hear that enough."

"I love you," she repeated, smiling.

"When your dad called I told him I was going to marry you," Joel admitted sheepishly, "and I realized you were the one I should be telling." He looked into her eyes a long time. "I love you, Emma—so much" He began pushing back her quilt and sheet, and she laughed when she realized he was preparing to lie down next to her. "I haven't had any sleep in two days, and if you can get jet lag flying from Baltimore to Iowa, then I've got it. But right now all I want is to hold you. Emma, your dad wants to perform the wedding. Is that all right?"

"Yes," she said, laughing, tears forming in her eyes. "It's wonderful."

"And I checked on jobs for bookkeepers, so you can do that in Thorn Haven if you want. Or you could open a store there—" He stopped abruptly and fished in his pocket.

"What?" she said, trying to pull him back close to her.

"This." He held up a blue ribbon and smiled at her. "Remember you said on the island that if a man were to bring you a present you'd like a blue bow for your hair? I stopped at your store and brought you one."

Emma threw her arms around him and pulled him close, and then she pushed him away. "Oh, I'm all germy!" she said.

"Never mind," he whispered urgently, hugging her again and raining kisses on her hair. "I don't care. I've got you now, and that's all that matters. We got each other through the storm, Emma. We're past the worst . . ."

Yes, she thought, clasping him to her. *The storm was over.*